The Pentonville Experiment

Lewis Owen

Disclaimer

Although set specifically in Ruislip in 1842/3, this is a work. Dickens wrote about the death of Jacob Marley in the opening to his magisterial novella *A Christmas Carol*, set in an almost identical period, this fact must be "distinctly understood" before commencing. There was, of course, a vicar in office at St Martin's Church in 1842 and although there may be general similarities between his life and that of my protagonist Rev. Edwin Carlisle, any other similarities are entirely coincidental. In no way is the character of Rev. Edwin Carlisle, or any of the other characters, modelled on the life of persons, past or present, from Ruislip or elsewhere.

Acknowledgements

As the story has a specific time setting and location, I have tried to be as accurate as possible in conveying the interior of St Martin's Church, its almshouses and the town of Ruislip in general. Although I have changed one or two locations, I am heavily indebted, and very gratefully so, to Eileen Bowlt's many hugely informative books and articles on the history of Ruislip and her people, especially *The Goodliest Place in Middlesex* (Hillingdon Borough Libraries, 1989). Until recently there was a strong ecclesiastically link between St Martin's Church and St George's Chapel, Windsor, and so I hope the reader will allow me the justification for retaining that link in a general way in the book. As far as I am aware, there has never been any link between St Martin's Church and Pentonville Prison: this is entirely fictional on my part.

Even though this is a work of fiction, I have, in my portrayal of the early years of Pentonville, included Rev. James Ralph, the inaugural chaplain of Pentonville, and Rev. Joseph Kingsmill, who later took over the chaplaincy, although I have been somewhat creative with their biographies. I have also included Lord Wharncliffe who, as Lord President of the Council, oversaw the Pentonville Management Committee before his death in 1845. In the sections dealing specifically with Pentonville, I have drawn upon Kingsmill's *Chapters of Prisons and Prisoners, and the Prevention of Crime*, published in 1854, and *Results of the System of Separate Confinement: As Administered at the Pentonville Prison* by his assistant, Rev. John T. Burt, published in 1852 (London: Longman, Brown, Green, and Longmans). For more general descriptions of the atmosphere and schedule of early Pentonville I have drawn on Michael Ignatieff's *A Just Measure of Pain: The Penitentiary in the Industrial Revolution 1750 – 1850* (Peregrine Books, London, 1989, chapter 1, 'Pentonville'). The characters of Harry Flynn, Mr Weathercock and Mr Clyde that are imprisoned at Pentonville are entirely fictional, although in places I have used some of the historical records documented above for the sake of accuracy. In one instance, for example, I use the letter of a real (and anonymous) inmate of Pentonville and place it in the hands of Flynn. In other places I use some of the actual words of Ralph, Kingsmill and Wharncliffe, and although I do not reference these in the text (purely for ease of reading) I readily acknowledge their source in the texts cited above (and encourage the reader to seek them out). I do this not out of laziness, but simply because I feel the tone and emotion of these words are so powerful that they give an authenticity and pathos that no creative author could replicate. I have also drawn briefly on Emanuel Swedenborg's collection of dreams in his *Dream Diary*.

Although set 175 years ago, the year Pentonville Prison opened, I hope this book will also have a contemporary relevance as we follow the journeys of the characters. I am extremely grateful to Rev. Stephen Coker, until recently Roman Catholic Chaplain of Pentonville, and Rev. Rock Sturt, until recently Anglican Chaplain of Pentonville, for welcoming me so warmly in a volunteering capacity within the chaplaincy of the prison. Furthermore, I am proud to be a trained mentor of the Feltham Community Chaplaincy Trust and look forward, not without a little trepidation, to shortly becoming a mentor at HMP/YOI Feltham. I would like to express my thanks to Stephen Williams, Community Chaplain at Feltham for this opportunity.

Prison reform is never static, of course, nor should it ever be and I write this in the wake of the Ministry of Justice, under the very able stewardship of Rory Stewart MP, returning control of HMP Birmingham to the Ministry after a period of disorder. I have been extremely fortunate in the past twelve months or so to get to know (and learn an enormous amount from) many individuals who, day in and day out, either from the inside of prison or outside its walls, work at the forefront of prison reform and education. These individuals include, but are by no means limited to, Faith Spear, Erwin James, Dr Andy Aresti, Dr Jose Aguiar, Dr Ben Crewe, Frances Crook, Phil Novis, Ralph Lubkowski, Dr Lee Salter, Michaela Booth, Michael O'Brien, Jane Gould, Jo Lear, Peter Woolf, Paul Delaney and many, many others. Organisations that contribute so much to this attempted improvement of prison conditions (for inmates and for staff) include The Prisoners' Education Trust, The Howard League, Clean Sheet, Criminal Justice Alliance, Prison Reform Trust... There are simply too many wonderful individuals and organisations to mention by name but I hope you know who you are and I thank you.

Addiction often remains inextricably linked with crime, and this dreadful, debilitating illness is central to the story. Yet, it is a story of hope, for anyone who seeks a way out of the perceived darkness and despair of addiction, regardless of their religious persuasion. It is therefore a great pleasure and privilege for me to be donating all proceeds from the sales of this book to The Forward Trust (www.forwardtrust.org.uk) – a marvellous organisation, who work in many UK prisons to help break the cycle of addiction and crime. My recent visit to Halden Prison in Norway, and discussions with various Prison Governors, have left me encouraged that a similar emphasis on rehabilitation rather than punishment may also start to prevail in UK prisons.

There are always ups and downs in any writing task and this one has been no different. It goes without saying that many friends and family have supported me. Tanya, Daniil and Sofia remain my rocks. I also thank my parents for their love and support; Alex Griffiths and Lee Oliver have read several drafts and offered many accurate, insightful and valuable comments; Julie Walker; Professor Thomas Dixon; Gyles Brandreth; John Leman-Riley; Felicity Morse; Johnny Hunt; Hywel Jones; Ruth Bitok; Colin Bailey; Fr Simon Evans; Fr Jack Noble; David and Linda Hudson; Janet Tippett; Maureen Tinsey; Gill Dargue; Clive Wallis; Alan Seymour and all the parishioners of St Martin's Church, Ruislip, who so kindly sponsored me on my run from Ruislip to Canterbury over Easter on behalf of the Prisoners' Education Trust and who have showered me with love in times of need. I am also most grateful to Rob Oliver for his evocative image which adorns the front cover of this book. Needless to say, any errors within the text are solely mine.

Lewis Owens
Ruislip
August 2018

Every professed Christian family would become a nursery for the church. Parents receiving the truth in their own hearts would hand it down to their children. This is, assuredly, the divine order. In aiming at this, they would not make their children less cheerful and happy. An infusion of religion into our home would take nothing from the real happiness of the young, but, on the contrary, give a permanence and solidity to their otherwise fleeting and evanescent joys...It is very deplorable that parents who have, through Divine grace, risen above the things of the world for themselves, should fall into a hankering after them for their children; and whilst formally teaching them sound doctrine should be communicating, in the way of table-talk, in which instruction is drunk in with the greatest avidity, principles which are unsound or maxims which are completely worldly. I know it is commonly said that the children of religious people are the wildest and the worst when let loose in the world, but I do not believe it.

Joseph Kingsmill
Chaplain of Pentonville Prison
1853

I will not allow the mental health of the Prisoners to be risked, as it appears to be now.

Lord Wharncliffe
Chairman of Pentonville Prison Management Committee
1844

For all the Tom Morrises, Alice Walkers and Henry Percivales out there.

My name is Legion, for we are many.

This is also for Neil Harrison and Alex Griffiths with gratitude.

PART 1
THE PREPARATION
DECEMBER, 1842

CHAPTER 1

Blessed are those who mourn, for they shall be comforted
Matthew 5:4

Reverend Edwin Carlisle closed the small, leather booklet, breathed heavily and looked out of his study window. It was barely light outside the Vicarage and the tiring, well-meaning autumn birds had long since entered into a deafening wintry silence. He turned his eyes back to the booklet. He was still perplexed as to how the diary of a man he had only met infrequently had been bequeathed to him. Duty and decency dictated that he had little option but to accept the unexpected gift, especially as Carlisle had presided over the man's funeral some weeks ago, but he remained perplexed. The recently departed subject had rarely attended Church, had little to do with community affairs, yet he was duly buried in accordance with parish regulations. The diary, where legible, largely contained nothing of particular interest to Carlisle: waspish anti-Tory rhetoric; personal reminiscences; financial concerns and confused philosophical ramblings displaying a troubled mind whose light of reason was evidently fading and soon to be extinguished forever. But it was the entry for November 11, ironically (or intentionally?) the Feast Day of the church's patron, St Martin, that had repeatedly caught Carlisle's eye. It read:

"There are certain individuals who revolt us from the very first meeting. Drunkards, illiterates, criminals. Society is no place for them. We have a duty to protect ourselves from these revolting animals, for whom a cage is almost too good. Society is civilised; these criminals are raw savage beasts riddled with moral failure and lack of fortitude and should ideally be drowned at birth. Failing that, shut them away in the asylum or into prison. Shave their heads. Soak them in carbolic acid. Once they are safely encased in this noble correctional facility, keep them in separate confinement for hours on end so that they can explore their conscience and realise for themselves just how much scum they really are. Then, when they have had the Gospel drilled into their contorted skulls and shallow minds like sanctified trepanation and their desperate sinful state becomes a part of their very being like their dirty, stinking, prison uniform, open the pen-gate and shove them out into a new, unfamiliar pasture in which to graze on twigs and wallow in mud, preferably three-thousand miles away so the stench does not reach civilised England and corrupt the pure and holy incense of the Church. Heaven forbid! The glorious Church! Out of sight is out of mind and we neither want to see nor think about these dregs of existence. They are incapable of redemption, rehabilitation, salvation. They have nothing to offer. They are beyond all hope."

Was this bitter tirade against criminality and the Church the reason the diary was left to him? For this one entry, which floated inconsistently between bitter anger, raging contempt and confused sarcasm? He thought it unlikely but could not fathom any other reason. He placed the diary back on his desk and headed downstairs for breakfast. The staircase, down which he descended, was broad and spacious, enough for at least three abreast, yet he clung somewhat nervously and unusually to the oak balustrade.

He stopped in the hall, retrieved the morning post and glanced over the government-stamped letter. He had been awaiting its arrival, its delay no doubt a result of the additional demands on the postal service this close to Christmas. Without waiting, he withdrew a small knife to slice open the envelope and mused over the fact that for the second time in a matter of minutes, he would be forced to confront the subject of criminality. After carefully reading its contents, he headed for the breakfast room and mechanically handed the letter over to his wife, who was already seated.

The room was suffocating with portraits, those depicting Carlisle and his father dominating from the main wall, hung with scientific precision. Deceased for over a decade, Carlisle's father – Charles Carlisle M.D – had matriculated in Medicine from Edinburgh University in 1781, joining the Royal Medical Society three years later. An attractive position at Westminster Hospital emerged not long afterwards and Dr Carlisle had relocated to London with his wife and young son, as he forged an eminent career as a surgeon. His proud eyes, captured accurately in the portrait, would follow you everywhere in the room, silently, surveying the scene. Two rosewood cabinets were chocking with different, unused varieties of china and porcelain crockery. On top of the central Georgian wooden chimney piece rested various smaller ornaments and family portraits. A bronze-mounted bookcase stood next to the fire, with its triangular pediment and Gothic glazed doors protecting volumes of Thucydides, Josephus and Tacitus as though they were strictly-guarded secrets, only to be allowed out under the strictest supervision. Towards the back of the room, a mahogany Broadwood piano sat in the corner, deep-red, dormant, waiting patiently for Sunday, when it would be called on to sing joyously to the hymns that followed the return from Church. The curtains were still drawn and light spread evenly throughout the room from two Regency chandeliers. The atmosphere was one of conservatism, of propriety, of measure.

Martha Carlisle, a rather dour and portly woman, had prepared, as had been her daily custom for the last few weeks in the unforeseen absence of domestic help, two hard-boiled eggs accompanied by bread and tea. Her eyes were dark after a largely sleepless night and, although younger than Carlisle, her face, half-hidden behind a morning bonnet, already presented itself as worn and exhausted. Carlisle turned his gaze away from her, as though in fear, and cut himself some bread. She paused, gave her husband a thoughtful look, and carefully read the following through her heavy eyes.

Right Hon. Sir James Graham
Secretary of State for the Home Department

Whitehall, December 16th, 1842

The Reverend Edwin Carlisle, M.A., (Oxon)
Vicar of St Martin's Church
Ruislip
Borough of Middlesex

My esteemed Sir,

I have the honour of transmitting my sincerest gratitude for your kind willingness to mediate between the differing opinions that are arising concerning the forthcoming Pentonville Prison. As you are aware, the prison is to receive its first inmates on 21st of this present month, a mere five days hence, the purpose being an initial confinement before their agreed transportation to Tasmania in the Southern Hemisphere. Her Majesty, and all of her servants, are extremely proud of this new corrective institution, which we trust most strongly, will act as a model to future prisons both here in the United Kingdom and throughout Europe. That being said, I feel I cannot emphasise enough to you my desire that any differences of opinion are to be solved with much haste. To this effect, I have also written this day to all the Commissioners for the Government of the Pentonville Prison, informing them of the kind and most welcome acceptance of your agreement to mediate and confirming once more the most fundamental facts already discussed and sanctioned by Parliament. That is, that all convicts are to be restricted to those whose age is between eighteen and thirty-five years and whose confinement at Pentonville will constitute their first offence. The period of imprisonment will not exceed eighteen months.

The practical arrangements and delivery of the convicts will be dutifully undertaken by my office of the Home Department and you need not concern yourself with any matters in this regard. Your assistance is, however, most actively sought, dear Reverend, as indicated in my initial letter of invitation some weeks ago, in advising on how the inmates are to be most efficiently contained within the prison. In addition to administering appropriate punishment, the aim is their moral and spiritual restitution. On this subject I am not competent to judge, but your experience and reputation at the St George's Chapel, Windsor, has not passed unnoticed and I have every confidence that your intellectual sensitivity and objectivity will allow a quick resolution to any outstanding issues so close to the opening of this model prison.

As agreed, I have informed the Commission that you will be visiting the prison for a detailed examination of the conditions on 22nd of this month, the day following its opening. I trust that you will be welcomed warmly by the prison chaplaincy, under the direction of Rev. James Ralph, and prison governors alike. It need hardly be necessary for me to add that any expenses that you deem essential will be met immediately, in addition to your agreed stipend for this assignment.

It only remains for me, dear Reverend, to thank you most kindly and respectfully for your assistance in this matter. I am of the utmost conviction that we all have the same goal in mind: namely, the smooth and efficient running of an institution which aims to rescue the most unfortunate and depraved souls from utter destitution. To this end, I am of the opinion that there is no individual more suited to assist than your good self and I rest with considerable ease in the knowledge that you have agreed to oblige.

> *I have the honour to be, with great respect,*
> *Esteemed Reverend,*
> *Your obedient servant,*

> *J. R. G. GRAHAM*

"Why did you agree to do this?" said Martha, placing the letter on the table in front on her. "I still don't understand." She was tired and irked that an already busy time for her husband (and therefore for her, too) was being unnecessarily intensified by this unwelcome request from the Home Secretary. She ran her hand through her prematurely greying hair and sipped her tea.

"Martha, my dear," responded Carlisle, with a tone that betrayed a little frustration and irritation, "we have discussed this now on many occasions. It is something with which I feel obliged to help and we knew that this request was forthcoming. And I *want* to help - it is important."

"More important than your own child?" snapped Martha. "He barely knows his father as it is and on top of all you are currently doing, including writing the 'History of St George's Chapel' or whatever it is, you now add this confounded criminal house to your activities. You seem to think that by simply reading that 'Three Bears' story to Peter every night you can build a relationship with him. He is not yet one year old but you already talk to him as though he is a member of your congregation."

"Martha, please," answered Carlisle, sighing and fiddling nervously with his necktie. He was a tall, gaunt man with receding hair which he parted to one side, prominent cheekbones, pointed nose and thin, pale lips. Given his emaciated appearance, if one were to remove his religious uniform and situate him in one of the many poor houses in the capital, he would not have looked out of place.

"It's a most dreadful story anyway, what with that hideous old woman," Martha added, rather forcefully. "I don't know why you persist with it. Surely there are biblical stories that are more fitting?"

"He seems to like it," replied Carlisle. He had always sought to avoid confrontation as best he could and sensed it was time to leave.

"Besides," went on Martha unabashed, "you are very aware that I have had little domestic help or nursing since Anne departed. Remember, Edwin, that you are now a humble parish vicar with a wife, family and responsibilities to us all. You are not serving the Monarchy any longer. Nor do you have the Church or a monastery to hide behind like the Catholics; yet you somehow feel obliged to play the martyr. One Saviour is quite sufficient." She sat back, somewhat regretting her outburst as she saw the earnest, pleading look on her husband's face. She sipped her tea again, regaining her composure. "Besides, you know extremely well how the Church are now not in favour of vicars holding several posts at the same time."

"Ever since we moved here to Ruislip," Carlisle answered as calmly as he could, "I have regularly travelled to London to fulfil my continuing obligations at St Paul's. I have never complained about that and the additional stipend is surely welcome. It is very little trouble to add Pentonville Prison to my list of duties. Besides, I don't expect that I will need to visit the prison regularly. I will meet them today and tomorrow and obtain as much information as I need to bring about a swift resolution. Thomas will deliver all services and duties in my absence. He will do a sterling job, as he has done before."

Martha raised her eyebrows, more concerned about her husband's unrealistic expectations than about the competency of his curate. "I cannot see how a swift resolution can be forthcoming. There seems an ocean between the two views from what you have told me," she said, cutting herself more bread.

Carlisle silently agreed. Although he wanted the resolution to be straightforward, he feared that it could be a protracted situation, and until he visited the prison for himself he simply did not have the knowledge to make an informed decision either way. He had met Rev. James Ralph a couple of times previously and was aware of his passionate zeal for conversion through intense religious instruction. Complaints had been raised about Ralph before, particularly during a previous post at an asylum in the East End, suggesting that said zeal was in fact a form of bullying and coercion. Such complaints, however, were inevitably and quickly dismissed by the relevant church council as no more than the ramblings of incoherent lunatics and hence Ralph's good name as a man of God was upheld. Carlisle was nevertheless rather surprised at Ralph's recent appointment as chaplain to the new 'model' prison and could, in part, understand the concerns of the less devout Commissioners, led by the aging, but still fierce, Lord Wharncliffe. These earnest, practical men objected to Ralph's vehement anti-Catholic proselytising and stern Lutheran insistence on scripture and faith alone. If such coercion continued, Carlisle pondered, it seemed that little provision would be given to prisoners for alternative, less judgemental literature. But was that not the role of a correctional prison? Not just to punish, but to reform, to educate and, ultimately, by the Divine Grace of God, to convert previously hopeless, immoral cases into obedient sheep for the Good Shepherd to lead into new and upright pastures? Carlisle was unsure. In the quiet, healthy air of suburban Ruislip, he had few dealings with serious criminality, except the disease of public drunkenness that seemed to plague all towns despite the Beerhouse Act of two years before, which aimed, unsuccessfully it seemed so far, to quell the vice of intoxication with increased licensing.

Carlisle himself had waged a war against the vices of drink. In the previous few years he had regularly condemned the 'immorality' of drinking on the Sabbath Day both in sermons and vestry meetings and even coerced his sexton Ephraim Ragland into traipsing to all the local public houses to report back the names of any tipplers who were also receiving parish relief.

"I will go today, as promised, and see how deep the rift is," repeated Carlisle, slowly rising from the breakfast table and standing upright. "With good sense and a fine lot of prayers we will make rapid progress, I have no doubt."

"Be that as it may," Martha continued, "I do urge you to remember your son, especially as we approach the celebration of the Nativity. I cannot fail to remember the story you tell each Christmas about the 'Eastcote Mary and Joseph.'"

Carlisle looked back down at his tea. It was no mere story, but a sad fact: over a hundred years ago, in early December, two infants, a boy and a girl, were found abandoned in a basket in neighbouring Eastcote. The mother could not be traced and so the vicar of St Martin's at the time decided to name the children 'Mary' and 'Joseph' in a poignant reminder of the Son who abandoned himself for humanity. Indeed, illegitimate pregnancies had risen sharply in the last decade and from the four hundred or so baptisms conducted by Carlisle, as many as seventeen were recorded in the register with the ominous words: 'father unknown'. Carlisle did not appreciate Martha's analogy with his supposed 'abandonment' of his own child, yet he managed to hold his tongue.

Kissing his wife, the vicar of St Martin's put on his heavy overcoat, which covered his loose knee-length clerical coat and waistcoat, pocketed a large set of iron keys, and collected a woollen sack of bread rolls, leaving his rather forlorn wife to console herself with the leftovers of her husband's breakfast and the pained crying of a baby from a nearby room.

Carlisle left the Vicarage with the sack of bread rolls and headed for the church, a brisk ten minutes' walk away. A dwelling for the vicar of St Martin's had existed on the same site since 1391. The current building, Georgian in design, had thick walls of rich brown brick; the thatched roof providing a home for the starlings and the holes in the outbuilding walls to the swifts. Carlisle liked the distance it provided from the church, a gentle descent with the River Pinn watching on as a silent companion. A frost had formed, and his shoes felt slightly less secure underfoot than usual as he arrived in front of the Church. The air was damp and there was fog hovering that cast an eerie light on the graveyard as he arrived and made his way along the gravel path. Surrounding him were the different types of memorials dotted around the graveyard: chest tombs, with elaborate gothic funeral urns guarded by ornate *fleurs-de-lis* railings; heavy, grey leger stones, placed low on the ground to deter body-snatchers and wooden grave boards, often rotting under the elements, for those poorer parishioners unable to afford the Portland stone required for traditional memorials. He stopped to pause, as he often did, at one of the many chest tombs. Stooping a little, he scraped away at the ivy that had crept disrespectfully and ungainly, like a lock of hair clinging to a clammy forehead, over the engraved name of Lucy Sherwood. A little way ahead, a fresh grave had been dug, the earth already attacked by the frost, and Carlisle's thoughts turned to the family of young Emily Marsh, who would be laid to rest shortly. The cruel, spiteful winter was no respecter of torment and grief and snatched away those whose constitution was ill-equipped for such harshness.

He could just make out the thin, bare trees on either side and allowed his eyes to rest rather on the green and red of the holly and yew in front of him, which reminded him that this was in fact a festive time. To his right, he glanced at the row of timber almshouses and sighed once more. They remained empty, unused, wasted. Since the closure of the Ruislip Workhouse four years ago, many of those in need of lodging and food had been transferred to the new Union Workhouse in nearby Hillingdon to break stones for the roads or pick oakum. Carlisle regularly visited to inspect conditions and had successfully pushed for a daily increase to 12 ounces of bread. However, he was acutely aware of many more still left without accommodation and on their own to scrape for food and warmth. Carlisle's suggestion to use the empty almshouses as habitable premises was not a new initiative: the house, initially built in 1616, had been converted into ten smaller dwellings a century ago for this very purpose and Carlisle's desire to resurrect such a service had been vetoed by the Bishop on two separate occasions on the grounds of funding, or lack thereof – "Send them to Hillingdon!" – and so these empty vessels also joined the ghostly panorama.

Nevertheless, although initially resentful of relocating, Carlisle had come to appreciate Ruislip, its church and, especially for his historically-probing mind, its mention in the Domesday survey of 1086. He felt it to be a spiritual oasis, only fifteen miles from St Paul's, but sufficiently isolated to warrant being called 'The Garden of Middlesex.' It was true that the church had fallen into slight disarray over the years: Father Time was unforgiving. The patronage of St Martin, erstwhile champion of the poor and needy, nevertheless provided additional spiritual gravitas to the physical bricks and mortar, away from the smog and grime of inner London.

Upon reaching the large, wooden door of the church he put the sack down by his feet. He had been bringing bread to the church for some time now, a weekly gift to those in need, prepared and delivered to the Vicarage the evening before by the local baker, Mr Paddick, but the exertion hadn't seemed to strengthen his physique. He let his arms fall down by his sides and looked back across the graveyard. Apart from the rustling of the red squirrels, which were barely visible through the fog, he felt entirely bereft of company.

Entering the ministry had not always been Carlisle's vision. As a child in Edinburgh, he dreamed of pursuing a medical career to emulate his surgeon father but slowly, almost imperceptibly, during his studies at Magdalen College, Oxford, his faith began to grow. Priesthood inevitably followed and in 1816, aged only twenty-four, he was ordained by the Archbishop of Canterbury and appointed a Minor Canon of St Paul's Cathedral. Shortly thereafter his reputation was further enhanced when he was appointed to St George's Chapel, Windsor, the spiritual refuge to the drunken and debauched King George IV and his embittered wife, Caroline. Carlisle had married Martha Wharton, seven years his junior, the same year, but God had not been kind to the newly married couple: three of their children perished in childbirth or infancy. It was largely this catalogue of tragedy that made him decide to relocate to the finer climes of Ruislip and accept the post of Vicar of St Martin's some seven years previously. He often asked himself what he would have made of himself and his career had he remained in London: Canon of St Paul's? Even Archbishop of Canterbury? Yet, though the couple had since been blessed with children, God had remained indifferent and the Carlisles were not spared further tragedy. His eyes moistened as he looked out into the graveyard and remembered his dear, dear, little Clara… only four years of age, dear Lord, only four years of age… Death at childbirth would have been more bearable. However, in those four years a special, loving bond had grown between father and daughter, only to be torn asunder just over one year ago. Her tiny grave in the churchyard was a constant and bitter reminder.

Carlisle attempted to snap himself out of his mournful reverie and took the keys from his pocket. He was surprised to find the door had already been unlocked. He stopped for a moment. Apart from a spare back at the vicarage, the only other person in possession of a key to this door was his sexton and undercover confidant, Ephraim Ragland. Ragland had occasionally, and only under exceptional circumstances, let himself in to shelter from the elements when there was not the time to return to his lodgings above the nearby *The George* public house, but Carlisle doubted whether the current fog would have caused a sudden need for refuge in this instance. Ragland was a tough, hardy soul, of Northern stock and would invariably work through the most inclement weather.

Cautiously, Carlisle entered the church with the bread rolls. It was naturally dark, damp, with no candle light and scarcely any heat. He shivered again and lit one of the thick candles set aside for Communion and then one of the oil lamps. The straight, long nave lay in front on him, leading to an elaborate stained-glass portrayal of the Sermon on the Mount, still in slumber from lack of light. In front of this window stood the pulpit and, to its right, the main altar. Stone pillars flanked the nave and it was a constant source of frustration to Carlisle that these provided a perfect hiding place for those of his male congregation more interested in catching the eye of a would-be betrothed than in his sermon. Two smaller chapels to the left and right of the main altar provided additional places for the younger ruffians to hide from the gimlet eyes of the preacher.

Carlisle placed the sack beside him and smiled painfully as he recalled how Clara would giggle and hide behind the stone pillars, calling to 'Papa' to find her, which he did, eventually, with an affectionate embrace. His eyes moistened again, yet he was immediately startled by the sight of a bundle in one of the pews to his left. It was evidently an animate bundle, as it slowly roused itself and a dishevelled head emerged from the largely thread-bare rags, catching sight of the perplexed vicar. A smell soon presented itself, too: a mixture of rancid urine and stale alcohol.

"Hello, Reverend." the drunken voice stuttered. "It's me, Tom Morris, sir. The sexton let me in as I 'ad nowhere, sir. The gin went to me 'ead last night, sir, and me landlord wouldn't oblige so as to let me in. I fear I may have caused a little bother. So, I came here, sir. It's mighty cold out there, sir."

"You are drunk, Morris," spoke Carlisle with a suddenness that was far removed from the loving and playful 'Papa' he had just recalled.

"Just a little, sir," replied Morris. "It's the gin, you see, keeps me warm, sir. And it was flowing a good deal last night at *The George* as one of lads had a winnings on the horses, so –"

"– This is not an ale-house," interrupted Carlisle, roughly extracting one of the small rolls from his sack. "This is a place of worship. Take this and head back to your lodgings now that it is morning. I am sure Mr Clement will allow you to return, assuming you are in keeping with your rent."

"A little behind, sir, but I will make it good," replied Morris, emerging almost upright yet rather unsteady on his feet and requiring one of the stone pillars for support.

"Please do not return in an intoxicated state," continued Carlisle. "Show some respect for the House of God. I have made this clear before. And do *not* lean on that pillar." Carlisle could feel himself flush and so turned away to begin placing the bread rolls in an ornate wooden basket constructed for the purpose of storing alms – a gift from a former vicar at the end of the seventeenth century. He read the engraving as he worked, mainly to try and quell his anger: "...bread to be distributed by minister to the poor every Sunday." Although this was not a Sunday he felt no qualms about loosening the rules so close to Christmas.

Carlisle felt Morris shuffle up behind him, the putrid stench unmistakable over the bread. Morris held his bundle of clothing in his filthy hands and hugged them tightly to his dirty jacket which hung loosely off his shoulders. Carlisle turned and looked down at his companion's fraying trousers, tattered shoes, sockless ankles and his anger suddenly turned to pity.

"I am sorry, sir," Morris offered. "I know I shouldn't 'ave come 'ere but I 'ad nowhere else, sir. An' I remember hearing once you sayin' that the good Lord 'Imself didn't 'ave nowhere neither to sleep so I was of the mind that it would be of agreed permission to come here, sir. There's many of us, you see. The sexton let me in, sir. He was digging in the graveyard very early. But I am very sorry if it's an inconvenience to you, sir. I'll be off to my lodgings now."

With these words he turned and shuffled once more, this time towards the large, wooden front door.

"Wait, Tom," replied Carlisle , leaning into the bread basket and retrieving another roll. He passed the alms into Morris' hand and smiled meekly. "It's fine. Take this."

Morris quickly concealed the second roll under his bundle, as if concerned that the vicar's sudden benevolence would be retracted, proffered his thanks and apologies once again with equal fortitude, and with a great effort opened the church door and disappeared back into the fog.

Carlisle sat down in the pew and looked vacantly towards the door, placing the candle beside him. Morris was right, he thought. Drunken, stinking Morris was right. Jesus did indeed say that he had nowhere to lay his head and yet I, a supposed disciple, have turned him out. The candle continued to flicker and partially lit up an engraving of Scripture above the door that Carlisle knew all too well: *The Lord giveth and the Lord taketh away.*" Carlisle looked down at the floor, thought again about his dear, dear Clara, and quietly wept.

CHAPTER 2

Have mercy on me, O God, according to your merciful love;
according to your abundant mercy blot out my transgressions.
Wash me thoroughly from my iniquity and cleanse me from my sin!
Psalm 51:1-2

Joseph Kingsmill looked older than his thirty-seven years. He attributed this largely to living the last five years in increasingly industrial middle England. The potteries of Stoke-on-Trent were a far cry from the freshness of his home-town of Kilkenny, Ireland, where his family still resided. Not that he could claim much allegiance to his birthplace now, except only in heritage. He had left the green hills of Catholic Kilkenny for Dublin in 1826, at the tender age of 18, to study classics and divinity at Trinity College, winning several scholarly prizes. Studying had always come easy to Kingsmill and he was awarded his M.A. five years later. An academic career beckoned but, pressurised by his overbearing father, he chose instead to serve the church and was duly ordained in 1831 by the Bishop of Dublin. Ireland, however, proved a little too provincial and too rigidly Catholic for his liking and he soon swapped its easy-going lifestyle for the working-class parish of Longton, Staffordshire, where greenery was replaced by grime, Catholicism by Anglicanism and Saints by Scripture.

Longton was a mere two miles from the parish of Shelton, where Kingsmill often visited (when time permitted) to listen to the powerful preaching of Rev. James Ralph. Although rather different in temperament, the two had struck up an immediate friendship. Kingsmill admired Ralph's utter devotion to the Protestant cause: only the Bible was the word of God and nothing could or should replace this divine agency, least of all the Pope. There were times, it was true, when Ralph's rather proud and haughty manner upset even the most hardened of his flock but, like his Lord, he saw it as his mission not to bring peace, but a sword - to turn son against father, brother against brother, sister against sister, in the service of Christ. Few tears were shed when Ralph announced that he had accepted a new post as inaugural chaplain of Pentonville Prison. His congregation wished him well, but secretly held a hope that his successor would be slightly less demanding. Some tears *were* shed, however, when Kingsmill made a similar announcement to his own congregation that he was also leaving to become Ralph's assistant chaplain. Some even tried to dissuade him. But the decision was made, and the proselytising Englishman and the gentle, academic Irishman left the potteries of Staffordshire for the human clay of Pentonville.

The prison itself was largely the brainchild of two prison inspectors, William Crawford and Whitworth Russell who, impressed with progress made by Pennsylvania's Eastern Penitentiary, became convinced by the idea of a 'separate system'. This system, where prisoners were placed in complete isolation from their fellow felons, was seen to be the ideal foundation from which to commence moral and spiritual reform. The idea resonated immediately with the two chaplains: quiet, but serious, prisoner self-reflection on their crimes and misdemeanours was the best way, in fact the *only* way, for the light of conscience to pierce through the murky criminal soul. This separation was to be punctured only by daily visits to the chapel and constant reflection on the scriptures. Any attempt to communicate or fraternise with fellow inmates would only serve to distract the inmate away from his conversion back to God. This would take time, of course: the human soul is a myriad of contradictions and a sentence of eighteen months was seen to be the optimal time needed for the chaplaincy to take the dirty, depressed and wicked criminal soul and mould it, by fear if necessary, into a state ready to be transported to Tasmania. There was no moulder of human clay more committed and effective than James Ralph and what was the concern if this process was painful for the inmates? They had forsaken their rights when they entered into crime and shunned the path of the Lord. Ralph saw it as his duty to not let anything hinder this purpose. Let Lord Wharncliffe and his fellow prison commissioners rant and rave all they wished about the separate system infringing upon human dignity and mental well-being. This was a prison and as the congregation in Shelton remembered only too well, Ralph had come not to bring peace, but a sword. Moreover, he fully expected his assistant Kingsmill (one may say his protégé) to fight loyally by his side. It was this rather charged atmosphere into which the pious, yet troubled, Edwin Carlisle was preparing to enter on December 22nd, 1842, a mere twenty-four hours after the first cohort of four hundred prisoners surrendered their lives to the 'separate system' of Pentonville and their 'salvation' to Ralph and Kingsmill.

As a man of moderate pace and, usually, equally moderate temperament, Carlisle was pleasantly surprised to have enjoyed the somewhat chaotic journey aboard the recently founded omnibus that ran from Uxbridge to Paddington. Although a London-to-Birmingham line had opened four years previously, the railway age remained embryonic in Ruislip. He had occupied himself with certain necessary prison documentation and took a particular interest in the newly formed interior architecture of Pentonville, designed by Joshua Jebb to the radial and panoptic design espoused by English philosopher Jeremy Bentham in 1791. This idea of panopticism supposedly allowed the prison officers to view every single inmate from a single, central vantage point. Carlisle smiled wryly to himself as he remembered again the stone pillars that prevented such panoptic possibility in his own church. Availing himself sufficiently of all required documentation, he then gratefully sought spiritual solace in his small, heavily-annotated copy of St Ignatius' *Spiritual Exercises*, a work that had engaged him since his university studies. A further short ride by the more familiar, yet not infrequently hazardous, hansom cab and he arrived at the Church of Mary Magdalene, Holloway Road, his lodging for the evening, sooner than he anticipated.

The events of the morning still troubled him, however. He was becoming concerned about his growing irritation towards his wife. He had prayed earnestly about this lapse in character but, so far, to no avail. The irritation remained. He had welcomed the opportunity to leave Ruislip, if only for two days, something that was rarely offered to any member of the clergy, and now lay, fully clothed, on the bed of his small room. He had been leaving the Vicarage for the church earlier and earlier every morning; too early, in fact, for any meaningful or practical duties to be undertaken: Morning Prayer was daily at 9am, followed promptly by Communion. He had taken it upon himself to replenish the bread basket, but he knew this masked the authentic reason, which was to have some time with his thoughts away from what he perceived to be Martha's critical eye. Deep down, though, he knew this judgement of his to be unfair and he was very aware of the real reason for his unease: the constant, unrelenting crying of his son, Peter, now twelve months old, which grated on his sensitive ears. Clara never cried – or very rarely. She was as placid as the sea stilled by the Lord, he often thought. Oh, but how he would have given anything to hear her cry and scream now – louder, more piercing than even Peter. It would be blessed, sacred, joyous music, but he knew it would never be heard again on this earth. *The Lord giveth and the Lord taketh away...but why dear, dear, Clara, Lord? Why take away dear, dear Clara?* He took out his copy of the *Spiritual Exercises* and opened it randomly so as to distract himself as quickly as possible.

Pentonville Prison, situated on Caledonian Road, was a short, brisk walk south, only one mile from the Church of Mary Magdalene and Carlisle, who, for the second time that day, had been forced to dispel his mournful thoughts, was grateful for the air. Passing the cattle market and terraced Georgian houses, he took a sharp intake of breath as the imposing sight of his destination came into view. Built on six acres of land, it was as though an external, concrete twenty-five-foot shield had been constructed with the purpose of allowing the imagination free rein as to the unseen happenings inside. This façade provided Carlisle with a curious sensation of both intrigue and isolation. The decorative gatehouse and clock tower, ostensibly welcoming, only served to reinforce a feeling of time gained and, ultimately, time lost.

It was fitting weather for such an appointment: damp, dark, cold and with no hope of the merest warmth until morning. A couple of fires had been lighted a little further up the road and a small group of vagrants huddled around the flames discussing, Carlisle imagined, their strategy, respectable or not, for obtaining food and warmth for the coming evening. He sighed once more and considered the sad irony of seeing such despair and hopelessness outside the 'model prison' into which he now headed.

CHAPTER 3

For, behold, that Jesus by the splendour of His divinity is putting to flight all the darkness of death, and He has broken into the strong lowest depths of our dungeons, and has brought out the captives, and released those who were bound.
The Gospel of Nicodemus, 7:14

Carlisle was rather relieved to be met by Kingsmill rather than Ralph. Although his previous acquaintance with the new Pentonville chaplain was restricted to a couple of synod conferences in London, where they had met only briefly and exchanged general pleasantries, Ralph's reputation had developed into one that somewhat intimidated the usually meek Carlisle.

"We cannot thank you sufficiently for making this visit to us, Reverend Carlisle," spoke Kingsmill, his soft Irish accent somehow matching perfectly with the copper coloured wisps of thinning hair. He was of average height, stocky build, but with a warm, ruddy complexion that immediately dispelled any sense of confrontation. Carlisle instantly warmed to him and after expressing his (honest) opinion that it was an honour and a privilege to serve the Lord in Her Majesty's new prison, he followed Kingsmill past the watchful eyes of three prison officers.

"The first inmates arrived yesterday," continued Kingsmill, as Carlisle followed at his side. "Not a whisper from any of them, by and large; as quiet as church mice. I think they were too busy taking in the surroundings, as this place is probably very different to anywhere they have been confined before. And even the lowest grade prisoner can expect up to eighteen months here before being transported. By the time they had had their personal particulars registered, been bathed, their heads shaved, clothes fumigated and prison uniform administered, I suppose there was not a great deal to be said."

Carlisle nodded to himself as he looked around. Despite the newness of the building, commenced only two years ago, there was a strange feeling of age, of decay, or forced intimidation. He paused and surveyed the corridor ahead, down which he was being led. It was hot, stifling, and he felt an inner sensation of trepidation and fear. As he found himself slipping further and further into the belly of this new and strange beast he found himself asking silently whether this was how the disobedient and lawless Jonah felt. Could only genuine repentance lead to freedom for these land-locked prisoners, like it did for Jonah as he was spat out? Or could it be that, whilst inside the belly of the whale, Jonah was taken to even greater depths by the grace of God and emerged enlightened? His biblical reverie was broken by Kingsmill.

"Reverend Ralph and Lord Wharncliffe are waiting to see you and, with your greatest respect and agreement, I would prefer not to leave the two gentlemen alone for any longer than is necessary. They rarely see eye-to-eye and as all cells are now allocated, there's no room even for the Judas Iscariot, so I do hope to avoid any kind of confrontation between the two." He smiled warmly at Carlisle, who could not help breaking into a little laughter, his first show of mirth that day.

The room into which Carlisle was led, on the ground floor of the prison, was a small boardroom of sorts, with a long wooden dark oak table flanked by six matching chairs. Despite its recent construction, a musty smell already hung in the air. In the corner stood an upright bookcase, home to a selection of leather-bound legal and parliamentary volumes. Directly above the bookcase hung a portrait of Her Majesty Queen Victoria, one of the many portraits that had celebrated her recent ascension to the throne. Her eyes, serious and steadfast, seemed to demand a change away from the noticeable decline in morality under her predecessor, George IV. Like the new Monarch, Pentonville Prison was to be a beacon of propriety: to set better, higher moral standards than before and woe betide anyone who thought or acted otherwise.

Ralph and Wharncliffe arose from their chairs as soon as Kingsmill and Carlisle entered. Carlisle recognised Ralph immediately, smiled graciously and shook hands with the forthright chaplain and his political opponent, Wharncliffe, who assumed an air of dignity most in keeping with his respected position. After the pleasantries were over, the merits of the omnibus debated and refreshments taken, the four men, who held the fate of hundreds of inmates in their hands, both now and to come, sat down to business.

Wharncliffe spoke first, addressing Carlisle: "You have received, I believe, a letter from the Home Secretary, confirming that we are adopting the separate system of confinement."

Indeed," replied Carlisle, extracting some documentation from a case and placing the papers on the table in front on him. "I have studied carefully all that was kindly sent to me and I do wonder of what service I can be. If you are agreed on the age of the convicts," he continued, glancing down at the papers, "namely eighteen to thirty-five years of age; first time offenders and the maximum length of term eighteen months, then all that needs to be agreed is the finer detail concerning what is meant by 'separate'. Am I correct?" asked Carlisle, addressing his question to all.

Ralph was quick to interject, and Carlisle was immediately reminded of his rapid speech and disarming intonation. "Precisely so, and if I may I would like to state clearly and concisely what I feel the role of the chaplaincy is to be in this matter."

"Reverend Ralph," cut in Wharncliffe sharply, betraying his own tension behind the polite façade, "this is, first and foremost, a prison. Her Majesty's prison, and as such –"

"– Her Majesty, like us all, is under the authority of none other than God," Ralph snapped back.

"Her Majesty's prison," Wharncliffe continued undeterred, his voice was steadily rising as he struggled to keep his composure, "has been established to act in the best interests of our inmates, to clip their criminal wings before we deport them to Tasmania for a new life. This is not a church, Reverend Ralph, with all due respect, this is a correctional facility and not all our prisoners will share your passion for the Lord."

Ralph laughed haughtily: "It is precisely because they have shunned the path of the Lord that they have ended up here!" "They are here for a variety of reasons," Wharncliffe replied, "some of which are purely unrelated to their Christian upbringing: hunger or that of their children; those with no education and the offspring of drunken parents. Many have had little chance in life. We must do all we can to equip them with the physical and moral skills to forge a new life for themselves."

Ralph laughed again: "And you feel that by letting the criminals secretly consort with each other during labour, and read literature other than Scripture, they will be 'corrected?' Heaven forbid! We have already been briefed on the ingenious ways the prisoners would communicate to each other in Millbank prison. They would not only monitor all the officers' movements but tap out nightly messages by means of the ventilation pipes. With effective solitary confinement such behaviour will be impossible, and they will have no choice but to communicate rather with their conscience. The very second their souls are distracted from the guidance of our one and only Redeemer, those souls are lost."

"I admire your verve for the Christian message," spoke Wharncliffe, "a faith I share myself, as you know, but depriving a man of social intercourse and labour is degrading to his individuality and dignity – degrading to his very humanity! We must judge a man by the size of his ability to reform and not by the dimensions of his skull, as many are want to do today. He must be able –"

"– Humanity and dignity can only be restored," interrupted Ralph once more, "by an honest and constant examination of conscience and reflection on the Word of God. Do you feel this is to be achieved by coercing him into labour, where the only lesson he learns is how to give the pretence of obedience until away from the eye of the officer and his lash? Nothing redemptive is learnt, except skills that lead to sleight of hand and insincerity of character – the very food of the criminal soul."

"As Chairman of this prison's management committee," Wharncliffe spoke up, looking over to Carlisle as though seeking approval, "may I spell out to Reverend Ralph and Reverend Kingsmill the quite simple requests to which we expect the chaplaincy to adhere?"

Carlisle nodded. "Please do continue," he spoke calmly. "Reverend Ralph, may I ask that you refrain from interrupting until Lord Wharncliffe has finished his address."

"Much obliged," replied Wharncliffe, before Ralph could answer, and clearing his parched-sounding throat. "The facts, and I stress *facts*, are as follows: The eyes of Europe are now focussed upon us here at Pentonville with the expectation that this 'model' will point the way to future prison architecture and discipline. We have four hundred inmates, with the provision for a further one hundred and twenty to arrive shortly. My commissioners and I share the belief of Reverend Ralph that a separate system is most preferred, although we differ somewhat as to the intricacies of that method. Until we have had a good length of time behind us, it is most difficult to declare it a success or a failure. Only time will tell. What is beyond dispute, however, is that the inmates are to be treated like men and never spoken to in a manner so as to irritate or annoy. Each prisoner is allowed to send and receive one letter every three months and permitted to receive visits once in six months, for twenty minutes' duration. Are we agreed so far, Reverend Ralph?"
Ralph nodded in agreement.

"Good," continued Wharncliffe, evidently relieved. "Food will consist of three quarters of a pint of cocoa for breakfast; four ounces of meat, half a pint of soup and a pound of potatoes for dinner; a pint of gruel, with one and a quarter pounds of bread and salt for supper." He looked up from his papers, scanned the room and continued. "Each prisoner will be expected to attend chapel every morning. Five hundred and twenty separate and self-contained box enclosures have been constructed especially for the purpose of preventing prisoners seeing and communicating with each other, even though I do harbour some reservations about such a draconian method."

Carlisle looked at Ralph and the silent Kingsmill, anticipating an interruption. But none was forthcoming and so he gestured with his eyes for Wharncliffe to continue, which he did.

"We therefore request, Reverend Ralph, that the prisoners' educational ability is considered fairly and hence that sermons are easily selected and hymns well-chosen."

"On these points I assume you have no cause for concern," Carlisle interjected, addressing Ralph and, out of courtesy, Kingsmill, too. Predictably, it was Ralph who replied, leaving his assistant and *protégé* in silence.

"No concerns, Reverend Carlisle," Ralph answered. "I am sure you will find tomorrow morning's sermon to be most fitting and accessible: Ephesians, chapter four."

Carlisle nodded. He had previously used that chapter himself to instruct his own parishioners on how to live a worthy Christian life. It seemed an appropriate starting point for the prisoners on their new journey.

"Prisoners will wear peaked, clothed caps at all times when outside of their cell," continued Wharncliffe, evidently most keen to have all items out in the open as quickly as possible lest his energy fail him, "again to prevent contamination of ideas from fellow felons. Ropes will be provided in the exercise yard which they can hold on to as they walk. Once more, this is a stipulation with which I am not in full agreement, for reasons of human dignity which I have already mentioned, but I am willing to proceed on this matter."

He paused to drink some water, looking as he did through the papers in front of him. He continued.

"Officers have been chosen carefully for their supposed unblemished moral character but will be subject to instant dismissal should it be proved, beyond doubt, that they are in an intoxicated state or have been frequenting public houses outside of these prison walls. We cannot expect to maintain discipline and authority if our officers cannot raise themselves above the immoral behaviour of those in their charge. Officers must develop a sense of feeling and pity for the prisoners, but this should not lead to overly familiar discourse with them. Any perceived instances of insanity should be reported to the relevant medical officer without delay."

Ralph responded: "I have every confidence that those chosen officers will fulfil their duty admirably and remember their obligation to God as well as the prisoners. To have no pity for the guilty and depraved is to have no Christian essence. The real Christian is himself a pardoned convict, lest we forget." Wharncliffe looked across at Carlisle as if imploring him to intercede on his behalf. Carlisle obliged.

"I believe that Lord Wharncliffe is implying that the role of the chaplaincy – that is, you and Reverend Kingsmill – should be confined mainly to the pulpit and the cell. Officers have duties and obligations somewhat different to yours."

Ralph replied: "There can be no difference of obligation in my eyes, Reverend Carlisle. If you would learn to hate sin and pity the sinner, you must go to the cross of Calvary yourself and see what Christ suffered for your sin. This applies to all us condemned sinners."

"I do not believe that anyone doubts our reliance on the Lord," Carlisle declared, "or that we are sinners. Nevertheless, I must sanction caution at too vehement an attempt to convert prisoners, certainly at first. The merit of the separate system, as I believe we all agree in essence, is that it gives the opportunity for the prisoner himself to come to an understanding of his misdemeanours and seek a new path in life. He is then at your mercy to seek further edification. But we cannot force people to turn to Christ."

"Neither can we coerce prisoners who follow the Church of Rome to change allegiance to the Church of England, as no doubt is your want given your previous hostility towards the Catholic Church and its adherents," spoke Wharncliffe suddenly to Ralph in a cutting tone, his energy temporarily restored.

Ralph erupted with a bang of his fist on the table. "Nonsense!" he cried. "Utter nonsense!"

"You therefore deny calling the Catholic faith the Antichrist?" Wharncliffe was now passionately motivated. He sensed Ralph's defensiveness, so he seized his opportunity. "You have been accused on more than one occasion, most notably in your role in an asylum, of trying to convert all Papists into the Protestant faith. Our list here is yet to be finalised but you can expect a fair number of prisoners recently arrived who follow the Catholic faith. I urge you not to usurp your duties as chaplain by treating the chapel as if it were your own personal congregation. Your role is to edify, comfort and instruct where necessary. It is not to convert. If a Catholic prisoner desires a Catholic priest, let one be found. Confession is healthy and good for the soul." Wharncliffe sat back in his chair, as if the exertion was again a little too much.

"I must protest most strongly," exploded Ralph, looking over to Carlisle. "In nothing I have said or written have I ever once described the Catholic Church in such disrespectful terms. God forbid! I merely pointed out the facts: the true Christian faith, as witnessed in Scripture, has never once purported to be a ceremonial religion, declaring an exclusive sanctity. Moreover, and as you have such an attraction to facts, Lord Wharncliffe, Joseph will confirm that the facts show clearly that more crimes are committed by Catholics than by Protestants. Joseph?"

For the first time in the meeting, Kingsmill spoke: "The facts do seem to support that assertion. According to the last set of figures, the rate of Roman Catholic males convicted for serious offences has risen from 170 per 100,000 population in 1824 to 326 per 100,000 today. More specifically, the figures also show that highest proportion of the worst kind of criminals in England are Roman Catholics."

"Thank you, Joseph," Ralph spoke, with an undeniable sense of superiority. "That is not the result of any personal prejudice but simply the facts! Consequently, I see no error on my part in finding certain hypocrisy within the Church of Rome, as they are more irreligious than even the most fantastical Protestant sect!"

Carlisle felt the need to intercede: "That is an attitude which I fear is not merited in such an environment, where we will inevitably have a mixture of faiths: Catholic, Protestant, Jew, Dissenter and many non-believers, I would imagine. I have much respect for the Catholic rites of Communion, rosary and the spiritual exercises. Indeed, the rich symbolism of the Catholic faith is one of its endearing strengths, I have no doubt. May I also remind you that Catholics can not only become civil servants but also stand for Parliament. I therefore urge you to temper your hostility, Reverend Ralph, and remember that we are all God's children."

Ralph smiled with patronising eyes. "I am very aware of your Catholic sympathies, Reverend Carlisle, no doubt influenced by that damned Oxford movement of Newman. We have all read his wonderfully inaccurate Tract about the 39 Articles. Simply nonsense. The Church of England cannot be interpreted –"

"– Reverend Ralph," cut in Carlisle this time, sharply, "I am unsure if you are suggesting that my attendance at Oxford at the same time as Dr Newman is somehow relevant to this discussion, but I see no relevance at all in entering into a theological debate about so-called 'Anglo-Catholicism.' May I suggest that we return to the task in hand, which is to establish an agreed principle of management towards the prisoners here at Pentonville."

"As you wish," Ralph answered, seemingly somewhat placated and not wishing any sanctioning from Carlisle. "I am of the utmost conviction that wherever Christianity, true Christianity, has been brought to bear upon criminals, through the application of the Gospel, good has been accomplished." Turning to Wharncliffe, he continued: "I shall consider myself, as chaplain of this prison, to have free access for all spiritual purposes to all prisoners except when they request ministry different from the Established Church. I will endeavour to be an ambassador of Christ and see my highest duty to be to discipline and improve the intellectual capacities of the prisoner, by education, books, and every available means."

Although Wharncliffe suppressed a feeling of doubt as to the genuineness of Ralph's supposed intentions, it was on this more conciliatory note that a relieved and tired Carlisle brought proceedings to a grateful close.

CHAPTER 4

Do not mortals have hard service on earth? Are not their days like those of hired labourers? Like a slave longing for the evening shadows, or a hired labourer waiting to be paid, so I have been allotted months of futility, and nights of misery have been assigned to me. When I lie down I think, 'How long before I get up?' The night drags on, and I toss and turn until dawn. My body is clothed with worms and scabs, my skin is broken and festering. My days are swifter than a weaver's shuttle, and they come to an end without hope. Remember, O God, that my life is but a breath; my eyes will never see happiness again. The eye that now sees me will see me no longer; you will look for me, but I will be no more. As a cloud vanishes and is gone, so one who goes down to the grave does not return. He will never come to his house again; his place will know him no more.

Job 7:1-8

We beseech thee also to save and defend all Christian Kings, Princes, and Governors; and specially thy servant Victoria our Queen; that under her we may be godly and quietly governed: And grant unto her whole Council, and to all that are put in authority under her, that they may truly and indifferently minister justice, to the punishment of wickedness and vice, and to the maintenance of thy true religion, and virtue.

Prayer of the Church Militant, Book of Common Prayer

Despite the closing of the meeting, Carlisle's schedule at Pentonville was not concluded for the day: a tour of the chapel and the wings from Kingsmill had been arranged by Ralph and as soon as Wharncliffe had departed, Carlisle followed Kingsmill once more, deeper inside the prison.

"It is now a little after thirty minutes past six o'clock," said Kingsmill, as they moved into the central part of the building. They were forced to listen to the many iron trolleys going back and forth along the corridors in tandem with the opening and shutting of the drop-down hatches fitted to all cells. "Prisoners will be finishing their dinner shortly, so let's begin in the chapel. They will spend the next two hours in self-reflection, biblical reading and letter-writing, for those who are able: literacy levels are rather low, as you would imagine." Carlisle nodded in understanding as they walked along the corridor, up a spiral metal staircase and through to the chapel.

"Reverend Ralph was not entirely correct with one fact," said Kingsmill as they reached the entrance to the chapel. "There are actually four hundred and fifty prisoners currently with us, not four hundred as he declared. The prison is equipped to hold five hundred and twenty in total and there are sufficient compartments here in the chapel to house them all. Even the Catholics," he smiled.

Carlisle looked ahead into the chapel and was immediately struck by the rows of box-like compartments that spanned the room, in a theatre-style tiered design facing a modest pulpit, behind which hung a simple wooden cross. In the aisles there were two sets of high chairs, evidently for the wardens to sit in authority and monitor the prisoners. The separate system was very much in evidence here and prisoners had little option but to face forward and listen to the chaplain, with any attempt at communication with their fellow felons prevented by the compartment walls on either side and behind them. Carlisle imagined that, when full, the chapel would look like a motley group of Mr Punch figures, with movement and appearance restricted to their upper torso only, their hands unseen. He thought once again of the old pews at St Martin's and was grateful for the freedom they bestowed on his own parishioners, even if, occasionally, they became an unofficial resting place for those 'under the influence'. He was nevertheless fascinated by these miniature 'houses' and took it upon himself to climb into one. His tall, angled frame sat uncomfortably on the hard, wooden plank and the only line of sight available was the pulpit immediately in front of him.

"As it's a separate system," Kingsmill spoke, standing in front of Carlisle's compartment, "they will file in one by one – in silence, naturally, save for the closing of the doors – and exit in the same manner. It remains to be seen how they will behave in such a confined space, but we trust their hearts and minds will be forced to concentrate solely on the Word of God. They will then be free to ruminate on what they have heard – Ephesians chapter four, tomorrow, as you know – in a brief period of exercise in the yard before resuming their labour in their cells. Tomorrow the corridors will echo with the tap, tap, tap of the hammer as they repair the boots provided to them. Soon we shall have them picking oakum, which will be a blessed relief to the ears."

"I should imagine that their cells will feel like a veritable palace after being in here," spoke Carlisle as he left the compartment and stretched his back. "I regret greatly that I will be unable to attend the service here tomorrow morning but, with Christmas upon us, my ministerial duties back in Ruislip necessitate a very early departure."

"I fully understand," replied Kingsmill, "and will inform Reverend Ralph. Your presence has already been of considerable assistance. Shall we take a look at the cells now? I am most keen not to keep you longer than is necessary."

Both clergymen left the chapel with its empty boxes and vacant pulpit, walked back up the spiral staircase and high-vaulted corridors, into an open space in front of the wings, where two prison wardens stood motionless except for the slight roving of their heads from side to side. Carlisle was intrigued by being able to witness in person the panoptic design he had read about on the journey from Ruislip. The design of the prison was radial, with four wings emanating from the central hub in which they now stood. Looking to his left and right, Carlisle could indeed see every wing and cell from his vantage point. He felt an uncomfortable surge of power flow through him, as though he had complete control over the prisoners' surveillance and monitoring. He was watching them even if they were unaware of it. He could understand the benefits of such a design: the prisoners had to behave *as if* they were being watched and as a result, the theory purported, they would behave well at all times so as to avoid punishment. That constant fear of judgement must be as painful as any physical lashing, he thought. Nevertheless, the feeling of human omniscience and omnipotence that accompanied such a design remained with Carlisle even though such attributes, he felt, should be reserved for God alone. He quickly reminded himself of the true words spoken earlier by Wharncliffe to Ralph that this was a prison comprised of felons and not a church comprised of his personal congregation. *Be still and know that I am God*, Carlisle thought to himself. Even in prison. *Especially in prison.*

"I will take you down to what has been called A-wing, Reverend," spoke Kingsmill again. "They will be done with supper there by now and although there are no different categories of separation, we shouldn't get any trouble from them."

The echo of the keys, trolleys and iron doors merged into a cacophony of sound and smell that caused Carlisle to wince as he emerged into A-wing. The corridor stank of stew, rotting potatoes, sweat and fear. On either side of the corridor, which was three storeys high, the closed doors were a poignant reminder that those detained behind were imprisoned, incarcerated, trapped. Unlike the former prison at Millbank, the doors here at Pentonville were to be kept closed at all times, except for attending chapel and the briefest spell of exercise. The drop-down hatches served as the only means for the prisoners to view their outside world and this view was only unveiled at allocated food times and at the discretion of the wardens. Carlisle frowned as he tried to remember the origin of the word 'prison'.

Kingsmill saw the level of concentration on Carlisle's face and decided to jostle him to attention with his favourite weapon: facts.

"We have all kinds of prisoners here," he began. "Soldiers, farm labourers, night cabmen, sailors, pickpockets, canal boatmen, prize-fighters, hairdressers, poulterers, waiters, drapers' assistants. But all with one underlying demon."

"Which is?" asked Carlisle, his mind still etymologically engaged.

"Drink, sir!" Kingsmill replied, almost with a note of triumph. "The evil drink. You speak to any one of them locked behind the doors and they'll tell you the same thing, I'll be sure: 'The first cause of my troubles was drinking... I developed a passionate desire for gambling and intemperance... A farmer gave me beer and I soon got very fond of it... I disregarded the Sabbath-day... I disobeyed my pious parents... cursed intoxicating drinks... infernal poisonous drinks... frequenting public-houses and liquor-shops...' I could go on and on. They will have time to think, to get the better of their passion for drink. I believe nothing can cure them but forcible detention from it. Poor fellows!"

Carlisle's mind immediately turned back to Tom Morris and he shuddered inwardly again to his rather ignoble behaviour towards him that morning.

Kingsmill came closer to Carlisle and spoke in a softer, quieter tone, his eyes indicating a door only a few metres from them. "Take him, as an example. Mr Clyde. Cell A-11. Hairdresser. Killed his wife, stone drunk he was. Struck her down. Without the drink he was by all accounts an indulgent husband."
Carlisle remained silent; Kingsmill continued to walk, pausing by another door. He smiled in approval at the silence behind it.
"It wasn't as quiet last night," he said to Carlisle. "This gentleman – a Mr Curtis – caused a dreadful din."

"Screaming?" asked Carlisle immediately.

"Screaming would probably have been more expected than the strange sort of music he was offering."

Carlisle frowned, unsure that he understood fully.

"He had contrived to produce an extraordinary variety of sounds with a small piece of iron," Kingsmill continued. "That, and the clear movement of feet in dancing."

Carlisle raised his eyebrows, still in confusion.

"Mr Curtis sees himself somewhat as an amateur musician, a frequenter of the theatres and music halls, and decided to reproduce such experiences by striking the iron on the brass, metal and wood within his cell. Quite ingenious, really."

"Remarkable," opined Carlisle.

"Indeed so," continued Kingsmill, "and with a most impressive precision of time sufficient for his purpose of dancing."

"All is quiet now, though," noted Carlisle, looking at the locked door with interest.

"Naturally, I was compelled to enter and warn him that if an officer, rather than myself, was to be on hand then quite severe consequences would ensue," Kingsmill smiled, moving along and leaving Carlisle still staring at the door.

"Looking at his records," Kingsmill continued, "it seems that Mr Curtis, prior to seeking fame and fortune on the stage, had worked on the railways and had witnessed several deaths and accidents through drunkenness yet his first temptation to the same sin overcame his resolutions. Drunk, he stole a cash-box from a theatre, was duly apprehended, and here he is."

"A Mr Wethercock," Kingsmill went on, now pointing at another door. "Transferred over from Millbank prison, where they foolishly let him work mending furniture. Took a draught of French polish for the sake of the spirit it contained. Naturally became drunk and maniacal for several hours, disturbing all and sundry with his bellowing. Luckily the surgeon was present and saw him to his right mind. His first words to me, upon seeing I was a priest, were 'I am more afraid of your coming than anyone.' Quite the Gerasene!"

They stopped outside the door of cell A-26. "Mr Harry Flynn. Amiable fellow, contrite and nervous. His history is a sad one, though, according to the records. A plumber by trade but from a child he loved the stable, became a first-rate rider, rode at steeplechases, bet heavily, started drinking and the demon drink won out. Brought disgrace upon his respectable father and sister, he has. Sad history indeed."

"Do you blame his family for his misdemeanours and current predicament?" asked Carlisle.

"Good Lord, no," responded Kingsmill quickly. "They are not to blame. What I do blame, though," he continued raising a finger, "is the circulation of pernicious publications in our capital. The figures show that there are close to forty thousand immoral and unstamped publications being circulated weekly in London. That's over two million annually! Even the most pious of parents have little hope against such a constant wave of filth."

Kingsmill gave a cursory knock so as to forewarn the inmate and unlocked the double bolt of the trap-door.

"Mr Flynn," he spoke, "no need to be troubled. If you could sit yourself back down on your hammock and continue with your reading." He looked behind him and beckoned Carlisle over.

"Take a look inside. This will be Mr Flynn's home for the foreseeable future." Carlisle moved a little hesitantly towards the open hole, his tall frame requiring him to stoop a little before peering cautiously into the inner world of the 'model prison'. Carlisle recalled the cell dimensions that he had read earlier: thirteen and a half feet from window to door; seven and a half feet from wall to wall; and nine feet from floor to ceiling. Flynn, a small, young man in his late twenties dressed in brown, broadcloth uniform, was perched uncomfortably on a rickety hammock which was precariously attached to the wall with leather straps. The outer walls of the cells were plastered and there was a tiny window, unable to be reached except by standing on the small stool that sat in the corner. Carlisle felt immediately the coldness and dampness inside the cell and shivered. Flynn looked up, Bible in hand, hoping with futile expectation that the eyes looking into his cell belonged to a harbinger of freedom.

"May I ask what you are reading?" asked Carlisle, with a kind tone of voice that he hoped would reassure the prisoner of his interest without giving any false hopes.

Flynn looked down at his Bible, squinted in the poor light, and then nervously back up at Carlisle. "It's a letter written by the disciple Peter, sir. The fifth chapter at the sixth verse; it was suggested by the Reverend Ralph last evening for wretched sinners like me."

"And do you find any comfort in the message?" Carlisle asked.

"Oh, yes, sir. Much comfort," Flynn replied, earnestly. "But I'm no lunatic, sir. I have a weakness for the drink, I'll grant you that. But that's all. I'm no lunatic. Never raised a hand to anyone before. The only hand raised by me is one holding the bottle, I'll grant you that. But I'm not a lunatic, sir."

For the second time in a short while, Carlisle was forced to remember Tom Morris and was struck by both Flynn's and Morris' belief in their own integrity.

"I have no doubt that you are not a lunatic, Mr Flynn, and I will pray that your time here will provide you with the opportunity to free yourself from the attraction to intoxicating spirits."

"Now that, I hope. I truly do, " Flynn replied. "It's not that easy but I do want to free myself from the drink, I'll grant you that. I tell my dear sister, sir, that if I had been ruled by her advice, and kept at home, instead of going to the cursed public-house and being swayed by others, I should not now be a convict here in Pentonville."

At first, Harry Flynn could see little benefit from being only five feet two inches in height. As time progressed, however, being a light load for the horses had distinct advantages. He began to put this characteristic to other uses, too: he was able to squeeze into the smallest parts of dwellings where other apprentice plumbers couldn't always fit. Before even his early twenties he had already travelled the length of the country, leaving his father and younger sister, to wherever the work took him. The family had left Ireland when he was a small boy and his mother – now departed – was pregnant with his sister. Although he had lived in London since then he had never lost his native accent or the repetitive, yet somehow endearing, quirks of phrase so proudly spoken by his father. A career on the turf beckoned for a while, but when that failed to materialise, Harry turned to plumbing and the obvious temptations that all plumbers faced when visiting numerous different homes.

Initially he was apprenticed by an acquaintance of his father, a Scot by the name of Duncan Baxter, a coarse, uncouth man who nevertheless had managed to establish a favourable reputation in the more affluent areas of Westminster. Harry's father had to pay rather handsomely, of course, for his son to be taken on and 'trained' but it seemed to pay dividends: Harry quickly picked up the necessities of plumbing and within a year was joining Baxter and his other cheap labourers on his regular rounds.

Harry never saw himself as a petty burglar. "My misfortune," he had declared when arrested on the third occasion and threatened with prison, "was to be placed among drunken men, when serving my time in to the plumbing trade. I remember well the night I paid my entry, as it was the custom then to do. When a glass of ardent spirits was handed to me for drink, I cared nothing about it, or in other words, I had no love for it, so I only took a little of it, when some one of the men said to me, 'You'll never make a plumber if you cannot drink a glass of whisky.' But little did I think that whisky was to be my downfall that night." His downfall was moderate by comparison to some other crimes. Due to his small stature and agility he was cajoled into various shops and public houses to relieve them of their cash-boxes. At first, it was merely a matter of grabbing the boxes, pocketing the money and taking himself on foot as much as seven or eight miles from the scene, only to return the following morning to share the spoils with Baxter. Later, though, and under more duress and whisky, his 'downfall' was more contrived: he would enter shops, put down a note and when the cash box was brought down would immediately seize it and take to his heels. To all intents and purposes, though, according to the presiding officer who had written about his case, he appeared a 'respectable man.'

Carlisle politely refused Kingsmill's offer to hail a hansom cab to take him back to Holloway Road, declaring instead that the walk was preferable. Although by now extremely tired, he felt the need to digest what he had experienced in the previous hour. Following on from Flynn, he had spoken to other prisoners who had differing stories but one underlying curse. Carlisle himself rarely drank; Martha never. He limited his intake of wine to the Blood of Christ and some occasional celebratory imbibing. Yet, turning to drink was clearly a dark, wilful cloud that hung over many of the less fortunate. He was on cordial terms with John Clement, landlord of *The George,* where both Ephraim Ragland and Tom Morris lodged, and was aware of how, for many, one drink started the slide into either anger or melancholy – the former invariably leading to crime of some sort, the latter to thoughts of despair and suicide. Since his arrival in Ruislip he had overseen at least five burials that had resulted directly from over-intoxication within his parishioners and those termed 'strangers': beggars, travellers and vagrants. He shuddered to think of those others of whom he was not aware, who had succumbed to the same fate. Would Tom Morris be next, he thought? This morning was not the first time he had been inebriated in church. In fact, it was quite a regular occurrence and Carlisle tried to reassure himself that this justified his rather cold approach. But was there any real difference between Harry Flynn and Tom Morris? Could it be argued that Flynn was actually in the more preferable position: inaccessibility to the drink, regular food, guaranteed lodgings and the time to reflect on his life and spiritual growth? Carlisle had heard stories of many vagrants who had intentionally committed crimes so as to escape the hopelessness in which they saw themselves to be.

Would Tom Morris and others like him be better off in the separate system of Pentonville than the apparently-privileged freedom of Ruislip?

Carlisle had thus come away from Pentonville with more questions than answers and had renewed misgivings about the effect that Ralph would have on the obviously vulnerable minds of the prisoners. He was also worried as to how he could offer any authoritative wisdom on the merits or faults of the separate system until it had been in operation for a good period of time. He would write to the Home Secretary to this effect, promising to keep a close, informed eye on developments but adding that time would be needed before any definitive decisions could be made. That would placate Martha somewhat, he felt, as it would clearly be logistically impossible for him to spend any good length of time at Pentonville.

He reached Holloway Road and the gardens in which stood the Church of Mary Magdalene, pausing to study the impressive building that loomed before him. He mused on the relevance of Magdalene: another reformed sinner, expunged of seven demons, he thought to himself, as he mounted the concrete steps. Arriving to his room he laid on his bed, watching the clouds scuttle past his window, imagining the current predicaments of both Flynn and Morris. Night-time must be the loneliest time of all for prisoners like Flynn, he felt, despite him being a mere two feet away from the man in the next cell. As for Morris' current situation, he could only guess: inebriated at *The George?* Intoxicated and frozen in a ditch? A refugee in the church? Whatever Tom's whereabouts, Carlisle felt intense sadness. Let Pentonville and Ralph be responsible for Flynn and let St Martin's and him be responsible for Morris, he concluded as he finally rested his eyes. Tomorrow he would return to

Ruislip and resume his clerical and pastoral duties. Tomorrow he would endeavour to show more patience and kindness towards Martha and Peter. And tomorrow, he thought most importantly of all, with the help of Ephraim Ragland he would begin planning his experiment.

CHAPTER 5

Then shall the King say unto them on his right hand,
Come, ye blessed of my Father, inherit the kingdom prepared for
you from the foundation of the world:
For I was hungry, and ye gave me meat: I was thirsty, and ye gave
me drink: I was a stranger, and ye took me in: naked, and ye
clothed me: I was sick, and ye visited me: I was in prison, and ye
came unto me. Then shall the righteous answer him, saying,
Lord, when saw we thee hungry, and fed thee?
Or thirsty, and gave thee drink?
When saw we thee a stranger, and took thee in? Or naked, and
clothed thee? Or when saw we thee sick,
or in prison, and came unto thee?
And the King shall answer and say unto them, Verily I say unto you,
in as much as ye have done it unto one of the least of these my
brethren, ye have done it unto me.
Matthew 25:10-17

As a child, Ephraim Ragland had been painfully shy. The youngest of three siblings, he had preferred the inner world of his thoughts – largely because he never learned to read to any great extent – much to the chagrin of his farming father, who failed to understand his son's penchant for pondering rather than ploughing. A bout of polio at the age of thirteen had weakened his hands but strengthened his resolve to fight for his individual survival and it was with firm intent that he left the patriarchal home in Yorkshire, at the age of sixteen, and sought the gold-paved streets of London. Various unpleasant jobs had enabled him to sustain his existence hand-to-mouth before settling down to regular labouring work with a family in East Ham for over ten years. When his services were no longer required, a sense of desperation beckoned, but it was a fortunate quirk of fate that landed him in Ruislip shortly afterwards. The Raglands were anything but affluent – simple farmers – but they were a large family and when it transpired that Ephraim had a distant cousin living in the 'Garden of Middlesex', he wasted no time in trying to explore – and, truth be told, exploit – this lineage. Cousins sometimes have the most tangential of relationships; yet, as the familiar adage goes, blood runs thicker than water, and a third cousin, quite possibly removed, had a friend who knew a church that was seeking a sexton. Ephraim walked for days to arrive at St Martin's, sleeping where he could find anywhere dry and, after displaying an unusual aptitude to work obediently and silently in all weather in one of the local farms, he caught the eye of the current vicar, Rev. Allen. It had taken Ephraim a while to feel entirely at ease with the physical maintenance work involved, but he persevered, and the church was naturally very content: he was relatively fit, certainly willing and desperately cheap and therefore was duly granted the post indefinitely. There was an irony in that he who had given Ephraim his new life – Rev. Allen – was placed into the earth dug by Ephraim himself not long afterwards. Allen's replacement had rather unusually started immediately, and Ephraim had served Edwin Carlisle now for five years.

Carlisle had assisted in finding him lodgings at *The George*, a public house a short walk from the church and Ragland had remained there to this day, his salary sufficient to meet the rent with a little to spare. It was, along with the nearby *Swan,* one of Ruislip's more appealing of public houses, close as it was to the Manor Farm, one of the parish's many farms, which employed a vast majority of its frequenters. Until recently, the publican of

The George had also run a butcher's shop from the premises and a greengrocer's was also on hand. Now, though, such businesses had developed autonomy and set themselves up in other sixteenth-century buildings to the west of the church, all of which had recently benefitted from slight modification to their weathering timber frames. As publican, Mr Clement had consequently sought to maximise its potential income by providing accommodation – basic, small and sometimes vermin-free – to those who could afford his entrepreneurial terms. Although nothing had been said to him directly, Ragland was sure that a 'deal' had been formalised between Carlisle and Clement for a long-term agreement at a pauper's price. If so, it worked well for all parties: Clement had guaranteed rent from a room; Carlisle secured a trustworthy sexton and Ragland had a walk of less than two hundred metres to the church. As was the nature of his work, he would often stop at the pump outside his lodgings and rinse off the grime and dirt that had clung to him whilst tending the churchyard or digging graves. He would pull the handle and feel the tension grow in his arm as the water rose from its source and broke through the rusty pipe. Despite the impressive depth of the well, which had been bored thirty feet into chalk to produce a shaft of over one hundred feet in total, Ragland never felt he was totally free from the earth. There would always be a fragment of it in his hair, in his unkempt beard or under his fingernails: a token relic, taken from the most painful of jobs, as the recently-bereaved family of Emily Marsh would still be feeling now to a depth much deeper than any public well.

Ragland's role at St Martin's was therefore a simple yet important one: to maintain the church and its gardens; to protect the inner chapels from dilapidation; and, most poignantly of all, to prepare the burial grounds for forthcoming incumbents.

Edwin Carlisle cared deeply for this humble, practical man. In return, Ragland had developed a genuine respect for the devout, if formal, Carlisle, with whom he had shared the most intimate and painful of moments. It was he who had dug the grave for young Clara last year, as Carlisle had wept and mourned. Martha wept and mourned too, but protocol forbade any deep outpouring of sympathy on Ephraim's part and so, as was his nature, he performed his duties admirably and withdrew, physically and emotionally, as best he could. He had often played with Clara as he worked, as she was always fascinated by his presence: "Are you a friend of Papa?" she would ask. "Why do you dig such big holes in the ground?" He would invariably change the subject away from such difficult questions and rather impart his knowledge of the fauna that dotted the churchyard with colour in the summer months and slept in the winter ones and leave it there.

It was with this mournful memory that he arrived at the church a few days after Christmas at the request of Carlisle. It was predictably cold, and a ground frost had remained almost constantly since Carlisle had visited Pentonville some seven days before. Ragland paused, as he often did, to view the grotesque-looking gargoyle embedded in the flint and stone that overlooked the church door and its ornate writing: *This is the House of God; This is the Gate of Heaven*. Ragland did not consider himself religious in any traditional sense, but he did possess a feeling of awe and wonder, primarily at nature, with which he engaged daily with pleasure, but also fear at human suffering and death. The gargoyle was, for him, a poignant reminder of the malign forces in this world and he had no conflict within himself about entering the House of God for physical and emotional sanctuary from time to time.

Carlisle was not yet present, so Ragland took the opportunity to enter the church and enjoy the silence. It was true that the church had fallen into disrepair over the previous decades and he assumed that this was the reason behind Carlisle's wish to see him here rather than at the Vicarage: to repair some of the broken wooden pews; to clear the vestry of dust and mites or to make the chancel look slightly more spiritually uplifting and inspiring than it currently did. He walked past the Purbeck marble font and slowly up the spinal nave, with its alternating round and octagonal columns that split the Chapel of St Michael to his left and the Lady Chapel to his right. Intricate wooden vine leaves and grapes decorated part of the roof, but he was always more intrigued by an image on the north aisle wall of a face with such leaves sprouting from its mouth. It was the mouth of the 'green man', he had been told, a common ancient fertility symbol, and he could not help feeling empathy with this savage face, so in tune with nature. Further along, another fading mosaic caused him to stop again: The Seven Deadly Sins, represented by a dragon-like creature peering down on him, eyes aflame. Carlisle had once explained that the chief sin was Pride, which was portrayed here seated on a throne, yet being attacked by a skeletal figure of Death. This image had always managed to soften the otherwise hardened sexton and since Carlisle's exposition Ragland had been keen to remain humble lest he fall foul in the same way. Directly opposite, as if acting as an antidote to Pride and his lustful, slothful and gluttonous companions, was a scene from Matthew's Gospel showing the Seven Works of Mercy, which included feeding the hungry, giving drink to the thirsty and aiding the sick. It was as his gaze was resting on this image that he heard the church door open and the vicar of St Martin's enter with purpose.

"Ephraim, I see you are already here," spoke Carlisle as he strode up the nave towards his sexton. "Do you ever sleep?" he asked with a kind smile. "I really don't know what I would do without you."

"Good morning, Reverend," replied Ragland drawing his eyes away from the image on the wall. "It's the cold. Never easy for me to sleep when it's like this. I get all pains in my fingers," he held up his blistered hands. "Better for me to be busy."

"None of us are getting any younger, sadly, and it certainly is perishing out there," replied Carlisle, stamping his feet a little in a futile attempt to bring them warmth. "You were looking at that wall painting again?"

"Yes, sir," replied Ragland. "I prefer this one to the one with the dragon. It seems much kinder."

"It certainly is, Ephraim, and whoever painted it three hundred or so years ago wanted to teach us something very important."

"About helping other people?"

"Precisely that. It is what our Lord did and what He called on us all to do."

"I'm not sure I know how to help people really, sir. I just get on with my business and don't interfere in other people's affairs if it's not for me."

"Believe me, Ephraim, you help more people than you realise with your most conscientious efforts both inside and outside of the Church."

"That's kind of you to say so, sir," replied Ragland, lowering his eyes with humility.

"In fact, it is most apt that we are viewing this painting on the wall, as it relates to what I want to talk to you about."

Ragland looked back at the image. "You want me to brush it, Reverend. I wouldn't want to make a problem with it, however."

Carlisle smiled again. "No, but look at the small image to the bottom right," spoke Carlisle, extending a finger towards the wall.

"Just a couple of darker lines, sir," replied Ragland peering more closely. "And I have always taken that to be a woman and child. Not really easy to see in this light."

"Those dark lines are actually prison bars, Ephraim," spoke Carlisle, moving slightly closer, "and I am quite sure that the two figures you mention are to signify the visiting of prisoners, in keeping with the rest of the image."

Ragland frowned. "I'm not sure I quite follow you, sir."

"Our Lord implores us to serve Him by serving others. If we feed someone hungry, then we also feed Jesus; if we clothe someone naked, then we also clothe Jesus."

Ragland remained silent. He always hesitated in saying too much to the erudite vicar, especially when the train of thought illogical and hard to follow. Being sensitive to his companion's unease, Carlisle changed tack.

"Come outside, if you will. I need your help with something."

Ragland rubbed his hands together to warm his fingers and followed a surprisingly sprightly Rev. Carlisle back through the door of the church and into the cold.

The church almshouses that currently stood empty were initially a two-storey building dating from the late sixteenth-century. This building, a private dwelling, had consisted of three central bays which were formed into large upper and lower rooms, with two smaller rooms adjoined at either end. Some forty years later, a conversion into ten much smaller cottages had occurred: five at the front and five at the back, overlooking the churchyard, and only thirty metres or so from the entrance of the church, where Carlisle and Ragland now stood. The Parish records of the time had reported that these cottages were to be used specifically for the purpose of housing the poor. Since the opening of the Hillingdon Union, however, the majority of the poor and needy had found refuge away from St Martin's but, like nature, Carlisle abhorred a vacuum and the empty almshouses had space which needed to be filled.

Ragland noticed Carlisle's gaze towards the almshouses and enquired: "Something wrong with the buildings there, sir?"

"Yes, indeed," replied Carlisle, initiating the walk towards them. "They are empty! That is what is wrong with them."

"I should know if anyone lived there, sir, but no-one has to my knowledge for a few months now."

"That is exactly the problem, Ephraim, and I fear they will remain unoccupied for months to come. This is why I need your help."

"I am not sure I understand, sir," said Ragland, resuming the perplexed face he wore in the church as they reached the almshouses and Carlisle withdrew his keys. The surrounding trees appeared to be frozen in time, unable to move in the coldness, as Carlisle managed, with some difficulty in the conditions, to prise open the wooden door.

There was barely any increase in warmth from being outside and both Carlisle and Ragland hunched over as they each sat on a wooden stool. There was a smell of damp wood all around them and a biting, piercing sense of emptiness.

"Do you remember when you kindly assisted me in identifying those of our parishioners who, though receiving church provision, were also succumbing to regular intoxication?" asked Carlisle.

"Oh, yes sir," replied Ragland, evidently confused as to the direction this meeting was taking. "I remember it very well. You had me at both *The George* and *The Swan.*"

"Splendid," replied Carlisle. "And has there been any improvement in the moral behaviour of the individuals you identified to me?"

"I wouldn't like to say, sir," answered Ragland. "I always like to keep myself to myself and haven't given it much more of my attention since that time."

"But you still see them?"

"Who, sir?"

"The parishioners; the drunkards that I had to chastise severely last time."

"Our paths do indeed cross, sir, what with me lodging at *The George.*"

"And I understand that Mr Morris is still visiting his old ways?"

"I wouldn't like to say, sir."

"Ephraim," Carlisle spoke in a reassuring tone, "I am not at odds with you on this matter, let me assure you. But the truth will help me greatly as I will explain to you shortly."

"Very good, sir," braved Ragland, evidently wary of saying the wrong thing.

Carlisle resumed his interrogation: "I understand that you enabled Tom Morris to stay in the church shortly before Christmas because he was intoxicated?"

"I did, sir," answered Ragland nervously. "It was one of the coldest nights so far this year and young Tom was a little off his senses, so I wanted to help if I could. I had only just finished digging the grave for Miss Emily that afternoon so was feeling a little sad, you know, and I thought I could help young Tom, seeing as I know him from *The George*. It's the drink that does it. He has one and then two and then he's had ten before he knows it and his senses have gone and he's as mad as hops. But he's not all bad, sir. He never harms anyone but himself with his drinking, though Mr Clement often closes the door on him. That's why I helped, sir."

"What you did was a kind and noble gesture, Ephraim. In that I am most sincere," replied Carlisle genuinely.

"That's kind of you to say, sir. Most of the time, Tom is in his right mind. His father used to beat him good and proper when he was a child. I often hear him cry out loud at nights, as if in a great deal of pain. I think those beatings must have stayed with him because he often looks as frightened as a bolted horse. I doubt he's ever even had an embrace, sir."

Carlisle himself looked pained to hear such words. "And the others? Alice Walker and Henry Percivale were the two other parishioners I had the unfortunate duty to berate. What of them?"

"I don't see as much of them as I do Tom, but I think they are still troubled with the drink, if I am honest. I think Miss Alice remains in the company of one particular man a lot. Not a nice man. I think her step-father and mother have as good as washed their hands of her and she no longer lives with them. As for Mr Henry, I don't have much to do with him if I can help it, sir. Rather troublesome, sir, 'specially after the drink, but I understand he is still in the employment of Mr Ansell the blacksmith."

"I see," nodded Carlisle.

"But if it is not wrong to do so, Reverend, can I ask what this is about?" ventured Ragland with a sudden concern. "I like to keep myself to myself and wouldn't want to be known as a gossip-monger."

Carlisle smiled affectionately. "You are nothing of the sort, Ephraim. I apologise for not being clear. Let me explain. I actually want to help Tom, Alice and Henry as much as I can."

"I see," replied Ragland, somewhat reassured. "I don't have any doubt that you have kindness to them in mind."

"You are aware of my recent visit to Pentonville Prison, which opened just before Christmas?"

"Yes, sir. Reverend Bell told me, as he was looking after all of your duties, including the service for young Miss Emily. Scary place prison, sir. I take my hat off to you, I do."

"Life is a struggle for many people, Ephraim, but that doesn't mean we turn our backs on them when they err, does it?" asked Carlisle.

"No, sir! It most certainly does not." Ragland paused, as though weighing up his next words. "But if they have done wrongly then punishment must be given, surely. Is that not the right thing?"

"It is the right thing. Absolutely right," said Carlisle. "But part of being a Christian is to confess our sins to God and for us to forgive those who sin against us."

"I would like to think so, sir," continued Ragland, "but I don't think I can forgive everything," his eyes looked towards the floor, with evident pain. "Like what was done to – I mean, if someone has done something really bad, I believe I cannot forgive that. You know, hurting a baby or a child or something like that. That is what Hell is for, is it not, sir?" His eyes, still looking downward, were full of tears.

"A crime earnestly acknowledged, suffered and lived through can be redemptive through the grace of God. But Ephraim, you seem troubled. Pray tell me what is upsetting you," spoke Carlisle, concerned.

Ragland raised his teary eyes and looked directly at Carlisle. "It's nothing, sir. Please do not trouble yourself with me."

"But I want to, Ephraim. Tell me. Please," urged Carlisle, leaning forward on his stool.

"It's just that –" Ragland stopped, composed himself, and began again. "It's just that I once had a little girl, too. Elizabeth, we called her. She was taken from us by a nasty man in London, sir, collecting young children in his cart. He used to be on the drink as well, we was told. Selling children for drink. I saw it happen, but I couldn't catch him, sir." He paused, his brimming eyes staring through the floor in pain and horror at the recollection. He gathered himself as best he could before continuing in a tremulous voice. "Elizabeth was found two days later. She wasn't alive. Not much older than your little Clara when she died." He looked down again.

Carlisle was startled, suddenly numb with grief for both Ragland and reminded again of his own devastating loss. He remained silent and Ragland spoke once more.

"I'm sorry for saying so, sir. I've not as much as breathed a word to anyone else before, except one young lad a few years back. Sometimes you just feel the need to tell another human being, doesn't matter who it is, it could be the most random stranger. Don't think it matters, sir."

Carlisle looked down as Ragland continued.

"I blame myself a good deal for what happened. I know a father's duty is to protect his children. My good wife's heart was broken too, and she never recovered. Died less than a year later by her own hand." He breathed deeply.

"I am most wholeheartedly sorry, Ephraim," Carlisle managed to say, tears flooding his own eyes.

"That's kind of you, sir," Ragland said. "She would have been a fine woman now, my Elizabeth, maybe even with children of her own. But I do often wonder if she and Clara are playing together in Heaven. That would make me happy. Very happy." He paused again, as if a world away in hopeful dreams, before that thought dissolved quickly in pain and he resumed in a bitter manner. "But, no sir, I cannot forgive that man for what he did. Not ever. Not even if he confessed to the Good Lord every minute of every day. It's our choices what makes us what we are, sir, not how clever we are. We can learn all things up here," he said, tapping the side of his head, "but choosing good over evil is what it comes down to. The man who did that to my Elizabeth was evil, pure and simple." He paused, seeing the look of Carlisle's face, which was a mixture of pain and astonishment. "Sorry for saying so, sir. I know it's not what Jesus teaches. I don't mean to cause you any offense."

Carlisle leant forward and tenderly touched Ephraim's arm, for once unsure how to respond. The sexton, seemingly embarrassed for his confession, rose from his stool and maintained a forced gait of uprightness and fortitude.

"What is it that you wanted help with, sir? I would be very happy to help if I can," he asked in a voice as normal as he could feign. "It's good for me to keep busy."

"The presence of evil in our world is a challenge to belief in God, that I do appreciate," Carlisle replied, in a soft voice and with a tone not altogether convincing. "But we must have faith. We must have love. We must forgive, as hard and as painful as it is. Anger and resentment create an all-consuming fire that will engulf even the most faithful in Christ. I know that from my own experience."

Ephraim remained silent, deep in thought. Carlisle continued. "Our consolation is that Clara and Elizabeth are now at peace." Ephraim flinched a little and with a steely look in his eyes, looked directly at Carlisle and replied in a firm, controlled voice.

"You know, I've never quite understood that phrase, sir."

"Which phrase?" replied Carlisle, frowning a little.

"Rest in Peace," said Ragland. "I see it written all over the graves in the churchyard."

"And why does that trouble you so," asked Carlisle gently.

"Peace, sir, is only peace if we know it and can feel it. If we don't know that it's happening, then it is not peace. If you get my meaning, sir."

Carlisle moved a little on his stool. "Not entirely, Ephraim. Perhaps you would like to say more?"

"Well, sir, let me put it like this," he went on. "Elizabeth could only experience peace if she were alive. But as she's dead I don't see how she can feel peace. It's the same with happiness or sadness. When you are dead your feelings are dead too. You can't feel nothing and so it makes no sense to talk about someone being at peace if they can't feel it." He looked away, the steeliness in his eyes becoming glazed.

"I understand," nodded Carlisle. "Believe me, it is an issue that challenges me every day, too." Ragland looked up again, seemingly pleased to receive some empathy.

"You do?" he asked.

"Yes," replied Carlisle immediately. "I do. But I also have faith that the real Elizabeth and the real Clara are now with the Lord in an existence that we cannot begin to understand. You see, our minds and senses are limited, Ephraim, and we can only feel and see parts of the whole truth whilst here on earth."

"That makes my heart a little happier, sir," replied Ragland. "I think I would prefer to think of her playing in Heaven with Clara and leave it there for now, if it's quite alright with you."

"Quite alright, Ephraim," replied Carlisle, still emotionally shaken by the unexpected discussion about his deceased daughter. "I only wish that I had all the answers."

Ragland remained silent and Carlisle sensed anger in his sexton which he had not experienced before. As a vicar, he had counselled many people from all walks of life, all of whom coped with loss and suffering in different ways. He would have liked to have offered a blessing at this point but he knew that Ragland was as practical as he was proud and so he decided to turn the conversation back to its initial focus to prevent them both from any further pain.

"I can understand that you wish to keep yourself busy in the circumstances," he said.

"I do indeed, sir," replied Ragland, firmly.

"Very well." Carlisle paused and then recommenced the conversation in a more uplifting tone: "How big do you think this room is, Ephraim?" he asked.

"How big?" repeated Ragland, still clearing his thoughts but relieved at the change of subject. "You mean like how many feet are the sides?"

"Exactly," replied Carlisle.

"I would say no more than thirty feet on all sides. Maybe a little more," said Ragland, beginning to pace all sides of the room.

"As I thought", mused Carlisle to himself. "And tell me," he continued, himself now rising, "how possible would it be to convert three of these almshouses – the ones here at the back, including this one – into temporary, private cells of thirteen and a half feet long and seven and a half feet wide?"

Ragland looked puzzled at the question and specificity of the measurements. "Thirteen and a half feet down this way and seven and a half feet across that way, you mean, sir?" he asked Carlisle, motioning his directions.

"Indeed," replied Carlisle. "It will also be necessary to darken this window to reduce any light from outside; a basic mattress for sleep must be provided and a small chair and bench for reading. Nothing more."

Ragland paused and took another good look around the room: "I would think it was possible, sir. As long as it is not meant to last too long – only temporary you say? I could build something, sir."

"For no longer than four weeks," answered Carlisle. "That is all that's required. Then it can return back to the way it is now."

"I daresay it is very possible, sir, were one to have the correct pieces of timber and joinery and a good few weeks in front of them."

"How long would you need?" Carlisle asked.

Ragland paused again to survey the room: "If it was just to be me doing the work, sir, I would expect a good six weeks or so, given my other duties, which I wouldn't want to fall behind with."

"I would like them to be habitable by the start of Lent, which falls on the first day of March this year. That would give you a little over eight weeks, and I will happily provide you with materials and additional payment from my prison stipend. Can you help me with this, Ephraim?" Carlisle was almost pleading.

"Sir, I am always at your service, you know that, so I am of course only happy to oblige if you think I can help you."

"I am much obliged. I have one further request of you, Ephraim," Carlisle asked, rather tentatively.

"Of course, sir," replied Ragland.

"I would like you to locate Tom, Alice and Henry and bring them to the church this evening at eight o'clock. It matters not if they are intoxicated."

Ragland looked surprised and raised his eyebrows. "I will do my utmost, sir, but they may want to know the reason and if they are under the drink they may not want to be in your presence, you understand, after what happened last time."

"Kindly inform them that they are under no judgement or reproach in any way at all, even if they are under the drink; in truth, quite the opposite. I want to help them and at the same time they will be helping me."

"It's not my business to ask questions, sir," said Ragland resignedly. "I will certainly do my utmost to carry out what you wish."

It had been much easier than Ragland had expected to locate Tom, Alice and Henry and it was a puzzled triumvirate, inebriated to varying degrees, who congregated in the church at the agreed time: twenty-eight-year-old Tom Morris; twenty-year-old Alice Walker; and thirty-four-year-old Henry Percivale.

Tom sat huddled with his arms around him, his familiar smell of alcohol and urine following him around like a desperate and diseased stray dog. Alice was of pale complexion and frail physique; a slight colouring and swelling beneath one eye testified to her precarious and immoral life-style and her matted blonde hair, unwashed for many days, hung past her shoulders. The remnants of a petticoat peaked out from below her long dress and over her worn boots that squeaked as her mean frame walked. Unbaptised, unloved and unfamiliar with church surroundings, Alice had been jettisoned as superfluous by both her mother and step-father who lived in neighbouring Eastcote. There was not the money available for both Alice and drink and she was, after all, twenty years of age and deemed capable of fending for herself. She sat on her hands in the pews to not only keep them warm but to hide the further cuts and bruising on her hands and wrists. She would return to the perpetrator later this evening and show her utmost gratitude to him in letting her stay.

Henry made it clear that he objected to being removed from his business at *The Swan*. A verbal confrontation with Ephraim had ensued, which was only resolved when it was laughingly suggested by other punters that the church had a good amount of communion wine which would not require him to break into his wages from Mr Ansell. When he realised that Communion was not on the agenda, a familiar cantankerous scowl sat on his dry lips, one nostril half-raised, which pushed his red and bloated cheeks into greater prominence. On many occasions he had come close to losing his employment as a blacksmith but, purely out of desperation, the aforementioned Mr Ansell had retained his services. He was tolerated by the local landlords but not liked and even Carlisle had to use all of his reserves of Christian charity when addressing him and the other two.

Puzzled on arrival, they became more interested as they listened to Carlisle's request that they assist him with some work for thirty days in return for free accommodation and food for the entirety of that time. This naturally appealed to the three potential participants who were often forced to beg, steal or, in Alice's case, sell herself for food and lodgings. The only conditions were that they were to adhere strictly to Carlisle's daily schedule for them, which would be different for each one, and that they should engage, to the best of their ability, in matters of the gospel, which he would share with them.

"This small book," Carlisle declared, holding up his copy of the *Spiritual Exercises*, "holds the key to a new life for you all. Of that I am quite sure."

"The Bible, sir?" asked Tom.

"It's a work by a Spanish man, Ignatius of Loyola, three centuries ago; a soldier, not unlike our very own St Martin, but with little education to his name. He started devising this collection of spiritual exercises, much like we need physical exercise, not long after recovering from a military injury and it is this method I wish us to follow during the period of Lent."

"Doing what?" asked Henry bluntly.

"Firstly, by daily self-examination of your souls and conscience," replied Carlisle. "Identifying your most damaging of sins, through reflection and confession, is the most important step to a new life in Christ. I shall also be doing the same."

"Will do my best, sir," uttered Tom. "Although I'm none too good with reading and that."

"No reading required, Tom," said Carlisle reassuringly, "just acceptance, contrition and imagination."

Carlisle realised immediately that such large words were confusing to his small audience, so he tried a different approach. "I want you to start, every morning and evening, by asking yourselves the following questions: Have my thoughts and my actions been pure on this day or the day prior? What is the gravest sin that is hindering my relationship with God? Do I acknowledge these sins and ask God to pardon me? Am I resisting the temptations of the Devil? Am I concerned only with my selfish pride or is my heart seeking a power Higher than myself?" He paused for breath before concluding. "Only by admitting such sins and surrendering to such a Power can we hope to be forgiven."

Henry sat back, folded his arms and shook his head. Tom spoke out again.

"Is that all, sir?" he asked. "I think I can do that."

"It's not all, Tom," smiled Carlisle. "I will also expect you all to attend Communion regularly. This preparation and confession are like dressing your soul for a feast with Jesus. You would not like to go to a feast at some great man's house without taking care to be clean and well-dressed, would you?"

Tom eyes widened with concern and he looked down at his tattered clothing. "But I ain't baptised, sir. Never been. It was my understanding that you 'ave to be baptised to do all that?"
Alice raised her hand, as though at school and seeking permission to talk: "I am not baptised either," she said seemingly embarrassed.

Carlisle nodded, as though expecting these concerns. "Technically, yes: only those who have been baptised into Christ are permitted to the Lord's Table. However, for the purpose of this experiment, I am quite happy to forego that prior need." Carlisle paused. "The bread only, of course. Not the wine." Henry scowled again. "I ain't never once taken the bread and don't intend to now. It's all balderdash."

"It is a fearful thing to fall into the hands of the living God, Mr Percivale," replied Carlisle solemnly yet firmly. "The Holy Sacrament is our spiritual food and sustenance and our petty excuses are not so easily accepted and allowed before God. I therefore exhort you, if you love and value your own salvation, to partake of this holy Communion."

There was a period of three, maybe four, seconds when the eyes of the Priest and those of the bitter blacksmith met. It was Carlisle who turned away first.

Questions continued to be raised, answers proffered and agreement finally reached along the following terms that Carlisle had already drafted earlier that day:

Tom Morris
Cell A
23 hours' separate confinement per day. No provision for work or contact with fellow participants except Communion. Breakfast, lunch, supper in cell.

Alice Walker
Cell B
18 hours' separate confinement per day. Provision to assist Martha with domestic chores for 4-5 hours per day. Breakfast and supper in cell, lunch at Vicarage.

Henry Percivale
Cell C
12 hours' separate confinement per day. Provision to continue with labouring employment under R. Ansell. Breakfast in cell. Lunch, supper at Ansell's/own arrangement.

Naturally it was Tom who raised the largest concerns, but when he was informed that Mr Clement was planning to give his room to a more reliable (and sober) customer, he sat back on the wooden pew and accepted his fate almost as a blessing.
It was a thoughtful Edwin Carlisle who returned to the Vicarage late that evening. Martha had already retired and there was silence. He had not eaten since lunch but had no appetite for earthly food. In the morning, he would write to Joseph Kingsmill at Pentonville and share his plans with him. For now, he removed the increasingly worn copy of the *Spiritual Exercises* from his breast pocket and headed for his armchair.

PART II
THE EXPERIMENT
LENT, 1843

CHAPTER 6

Like as a father pitieth his children,
so the Lord pitieth them that fear him.
For he knoweth our frame; he remembereth that we are dust.
As for man, his days are as grass:
as a flower of the field, do he flourisheth
For the wind passeth over it, and it is gone:
and the place thereof shall know it no more.
Psalm 103:13-17

Reverend Edwin Carlisle, M.A. Oxon
St Martin's Church Vicarage
Borough of Middlesex
December 30th, 1842

Reverend Joseph Kingsmill
Chaplain
HMP Pentonville
Caledonian Road
London

My esteemed Reverend Kingsmill,

May I begin by relaying the utmost pleasure I received in meeting you during my recent visit to Pentonville Prison. The kindness that you and Reverend Ralph bestowed upon me was of the highest order and I remain entirely indebted to you. I left Pentonville both more informed and relieved as to its future benefit for our prisoners' welfare, physically and spiritually, and I have no question in my mind that you will prove to be a shining light to fellow countries and institutions. I will, immediately on completion of this present letter to you, write to Mr Graham at the Home Department and convey the outcome of my visit which, I can assure you, will display you in a most favourable light. My duties here at Ruislip and elsewhere will, sadly, prevent me from visiting you at Pentonville in a frequency I would welcome, although I hope to visit you again in the coming months. I see no reason, following our most productive meeting with Lord Wharncliffe, for me to intrude on your important work further at this time. I pray that God may give you the strength and guidance to undertake and fulfil your duties to the praise and glory of His name.

May I also, at this opportunity, inform you of my forthcoming plans here at St Martin's Church which, I trust, will be of interest to you and Reverend Ralph. Since my visit to Pentonville I have, naturally, given much thought to the merits of the 'separate system'. Furthermore, the evident malign influence of intoxicating drinks, which you so vividly relayed to me, is not without presence here among our more desperate parishioners. I have therefore set before me an experiment (though not in any formal sense), whereby I will be replicating the individual confinement at Pentonville, as best as circumstances and premises allow, on three of our most needy parishioners for whom the drink is a constant demon in their lives. They will reside in temporary 'cells' next to the church and I will endeavour to guide them on a journey of discipline and self-reflection, following the most noble Spiritual Exercises of Ignatius of Loyola, a work with which, I have no doubt, you are extremely familiar. Though none of my 'prisoners' (I use that term most lightly) have committed any crime of which I am aware, I wish to see how the 'separate system' (in different degrees) will help them to tackle their poisoned minds in respect to sinfulness and intoxication. All three subjects have agreed to engage in this rather unorthodox but important experiment. I have set for them a daily routine based on the recommended thirty-day schedule of the Spiritual Exercises and as close to the daily structure of the prison that I could muster.

This will commence on the first day of March (the beginning of Lent) and terminate on the closing day of the same month. My sexton will kindly be assisting me with the daily provision and delivery of meals. Two of the participants will be engaged in different levels of labour; the remaining participant will be subject to the prolonged confinement that you employ at the prison. I have no prophetic insight into how such an experiment will proceed and of course the circumstances and surroundings cannot match those of Pentonville in any true sense. Nevertheless, I have a strong hope that I can facilitate a much-needed development of conscience and repentance which, I pray, will lead these troubled souls into the light of redemption and freedom from drunkenness.

I plan to maintain a journal and will, with the greatest pleasure, keep you abreast of how things progress. In return, I would be most grateful if you could likewise keep me informed of the progress of certain prisoners under the 'separate system' in your care – in particular Mr Harry Flynn, to whom my heart went out more than to others.

It only remains for me to offer my sincerest gratitude once more and to offer my heartfelt blessings to you and Reverend Ralph.

I remain,

yours most sincerely,

Reverend Edwin Carlisle

**

Reverend Joseph Kingsmill
Chaplain
HMP Pentonville
Caledonian Road
London
January 9th, 1843

Reverend Edwin Carlisle, M.A. Oxon
St Martin's Church Vicarage
Borough of Middlesex
December 30th, 1842

My dear Reverend Carlisle,
It was a great delight to receive your letter. I can assure you that the pleasure was very much mine and Reverend Ralph's following your visit here to Pentonville.

It has been a relatively smooth commencement to life here. There has been little cause for concern among the prisoners, except for the expected rebellious behaviour of one or two, which was quickly subdued and finally quelled. Likewise, a case of mental instability concerning Mr Weathercock was rapidly addressed and he is now safely in his cell after a period of medical supervision. As with a sinking ship, we must first stop the leak before any examination of the cause can occur. Attendance at chapel has been consistently at a high level and I can witness to the fact that Reverend Ralph's methods – strict though they are – are bearing initial fruit. The separate system does indeed seem to give the prisoners the time and space to reflect on their past misdemeanours and to absorb, as best their intelligence can, the various scriptural expositions and lessons with which we provide them. Condemnation rarely leads to liberation.

Mr Harry Flynn, whom you mention in your previous letter, is one such prisoner who seems to be embracing our method with generally positive results. By and large he remains a quiet, thoughtful individual, who spends his waking hours most productively by examining the Scripture and his conscience. I have hopes that he will not only be reformed but will see the light of God's Love and become a 'new creation in Christ.' We must continue to provide those within our care with kindness: we cannot beat them into submission to Christ. We must remember that depression of spirits is not contrition; remorse is not repentance; resolutions and vows of amendment, made whilst suffering the penalty of transgression, imply no change of principle, - no real reformation of character. The weakening of man's physical and mental energies does not generate piety. Religion cannot be in a healthy state which originates in the disturbance of the mental powers. On this, I am quite sure, we are in complete agreement.

Now to your most fascinating experiment! I do not know where to begin! It suffices for me to say that it is a most ingenious idea! I am indeed very familiar with the Spiritual Exercises (a work I studied most carefully in my student days back in Ireland) and it is a text of the utmost practicality and importance, as you know so well yourself. I am most intrigued to see how your participants progress, not knowing them personally, of course. I pray that you keep me informed of how your 'experiment' proceeds and if you have any experiences that you feel may benefit our own work here at Pentonville, please do inform us.

I write this letter with the utmost respect and anticipation as to your future news. I will keep you in my prayers and ask that God may keep you safe.

Your servant in Christ,

J. Kingsmill

The three months prior to the start of Carlisle's experiment had been unremarkable yet productive. It had, however, taken him longer than he hoped to convince Martha that a twenty-year-old unbaptised prostitute would be a useful addition to their domestic life. Initially, Martha was horrified and refused unconditionally to allow Alice to assist her. Slowly, though, over the weeks and her growing frustration at her husband's continued lack of engagement with their son, she began to yearn not only for practical assistance but also female companionship. There were of course parishioners with whom she could talk and in whom she could confide, but she knew all-too-well that one never truly trusts the wife of a vicar, so there was something quite appealing about an outsider sharing her daily life. It was only four hours a day, she told herself, and that extra help would indeed be welcome. So, eventually, she warmed to the idea and gave Carlisle her blessing.

Also during this time, Ephraim Ragland had busied himself with the construction of the almshouses into temporary cells, in strict accordance with the measurements laid out by Carlisle to replicate those of Pentonville. The cells were by no means perfect: the timber partitions were firm but liable to creak slightly in the wind and the makeshift beds were balanced precariously on one side of the wall but, on completion, they resembled a prison cell as well as could have been expected in the time and materials provided.

Tom Morris had managed to persuade Mr Clement to keep his room until March 1, when he would move into this temporary accommodation but after that he was on his own - Mr Clement had been most adamant about that. Carlisle was somewhat disappointed at Clement's ruthlessness, but he was well aware that Morris had often failed to meet his rent whilst his drinking took control. On three or four occasions since Christmas, Morris had also turned up to Communion drunk again and, whilst always seated at the rear, apologetic and never confrontational, had caused growing consternation among the more privileged parishioners. Nevertheless, there was something endearing about his apparent hopelessness that made Carlisle even more determined to help. Not the same could be said, if truth be told, about Henry Percivale, who continued to be a most cantankerous individual, especially when 'under the influence'. Ephraim had reported to Carlisle that quite frequently Percivale had been either the instigator or the recipient of a physical confrontation with a fellow imbiber at *The Swan*. Matters were further complicated by a visit from his employer Mr Ansell, who confessed his growing unease about retaining his employee on his books and which reminded Carlisle just how much of a challenge it would be to steer Percivale into a new direction in life.

March 1 arrived and the first day of Spring was greeted with rain. Carlisle was more than a little apprehensive as he left the Vicarage and embarked upon his usual walk towards the church. He had announced his plans to his parishioners some weeks before and had focussed his last two sermons on the need for the Church to embrace sinners. Fortunately, he had been met only with raised eyebrows rather than active resistance and the three participants had arrived the evening before and had now become resident in their cells. They were drunk except Alice, who appeared sporting a further facial abrasion, no doubt a leaving present from her abandoned landlord. Percivale complained repeatedly and inevitably, spitting out a tirade of unwelcome filth upon his arrival, but when Carlisle politely but firmly reminded him that Mr Ansell had insisted on regular updates in order for his employment to be maintained, he threw his belongings into one corner of his room and scowled like a chastised child as Carlisle locked him in.

Carlisle had given them the schedule for the day the previous evening and, after a small breakfast which Martha had prepared, he was expecting all three to attend Morning Prayer at 9am and Communion thereafter. Ragland would be on hand to rouse them if required, providing them with water and a bucket for washing, leaving Carlisle to prepare for his usual morning ministerial duties. Following on from these duties, Carlisle would then engage all three in the first sessions of what the *Spiritual Exercises* referred to as *The Examen*: an honest and searching examination of their sins and vices. He would spend no more than thirty minutes with each of them before reading a passage of Scripture on which to reflect. Alice would then depart for the Vicarage to assist Martha, Henry for Mr Ansell's horses, and Tom to remain in his cell, accompanied only by his thoughts. In the afternoon following lunch, which would be administered to Tom by Ragland, to Alice by Martha and to Henry by Ansell, a further period of *examen* would take place accompanied by more Scripture and reflection. The evening period, after supper in their cells, would be largely for reflection on the day and the chance for Carlisle to write his Journal, privately, which he would keep locked in the drawer of his study desk.

At first, Ragland had struggled to grasp the essence of the experiment with which he was assisting. Carlisle had explained, as best he could and in general terms, that the aim was to bring about a conversion or change of heart through discernment of good thoughts and actions.

"We have a splendid opportunity to help these people, Ephraim," Carlisle had said, "to get rid of all their darkness and turn it into light."

Ragland had doubts that such an approach would make any headway with individuals as saturated in anger as Percivale.

"These are very troubled souls, sir. Very troubled indeed. They no trust no one. Not even their own selves," he had responded.

"Then I must teach them first to trust others and ultimately, as Ignatius himself says, to 'conquer themselves,'" Carlisle replied.

"They may not want to be conquered, sir. That's all I am saying," Ephraim retorted. "They ain't had it easy growing up and they just want to survive, sir. Nothing more than that.

"In which case, we must help them to remove their pretence of toughness, Ephraim! Take off their masks and embrace them with the love of Christ."

"I can't see how twenty or more years of hell will be made better in four weeks, if I may say so, sir. Too much has happened to them. But as you wish."

"I do not proclaim for one minute that any results will be immediate, Ephraim," Carlisle added, growing a little frustrated with Ragland's obstructions. "Nevertheless, if I provide them with a safe space where they can reflect on their past and their current difficulties then I am sure the light of God will form within them. I will get them to confess their deepest sins, nail them to the cross and then burn them. Their sins and their hatred will be nothing but ashes; fertiliser for new soil. Surely there is nothing to lose?"

"They are not animals, sir. They are humans, with feelings and fears. Just like you and me. Sometimes the past is left well alone." Carlisle paused a little before replying.

"You know the story of the eagle egg that was hatched amongst chickens, Ephraim?"

"I don't believe I do, sir."

"Well, the eagle grew up all of its life thinking it was a chicken! It clucked day and night like all of the others and died not knowing that it possessed the ability to fly."

"And what is your meaning, sir?" asked Ragland.

"I mean that I want Tom, Alice and Henry to realise their wings. To fly above the despair into which they have fallen. That, Ephraim, is my duty as a Christian minister."

"Sometimes chickens are happy being chickens, sir. They are quite happy clucking away in their own company. Just my thoughts, that's all. But, like I say, as you wish."

Ragland continued to struggle to understand *why* all three participants would agree to such an experiment. As was his way, though, he respectfully agreed to all duties bestowed upon him. Carlisle had retained regular correspondence with Joseph Kingsmill at Pentonville and was disheartened by news of Harry Flynn who was, according to Kingsmill 'no longer a model prisoner inside a model prison.' Flynn, it seemed evident from Kingsmill's most recent letter, was now finding the effects of separate confinement very severe and, although only a matter of months into his eighteen-month sentence, was complaining bitterly about headaches and attacks of fear at night. Kingsmill reported how, on several occasions, Flynn had demanded attention at his cell as a matter of urgency, only to enquire as to the time of day, 'as though he just wanted to know that another human voice was interested in what he had to say.' Maybe that *is* a matter of urgency to him, reflected Kingsmill in his letter, further reporting that Ralph's official line was that Flynn's priority was to 'use his time to reflect on his pending eternity.' Not wishing to interfere unduly, Carlisle had subsequently, and as planned, written to the Home Secretary outlining that his observation 'from a distance' was the most suitable option for now, but he did intend to visit the prison again after Easter.

On this particular morning, therefore, Carlisle was again grateful for the distance between the Vicarage and the church, which provided him with the space to expel any thoughts that may have hindered the task in hand. As the rain continued, these thoughts switched to Peter, growing stronger and more vocal by the day. Under duress from Martha, Carlisle had stopped reading the Three Bears' story and instead had begun using a small, tattered book of children's Bible stories, which his own father had patiently read to him over forty years ago. Peter appeared to listen contently; Carlisle, however, found his academically-trained mind increasingly questioning the meaning of the stories he was relaying: could anyone but a child really believe these stories to be true? And if, for example, the story of Noah was symbolic, what other stories were also factually false? Adam and Eve? David and Goliath? The Virgin Birth? The raising of Lazarus? The resurrection of Christ Himself? How can something symbolic also be verifiably true? He stopped himself at this point and cursed himself.

He had become aware of subtle changes in his faith over the last few months: more questioning, less accepting and increasingly sceptical. He had inherited his rational, scientific mind from his medical father and allowed himself little room for myth and symbolism. He had also experienced a perceptible change in his feelings towards Alice as the time drew near for the experiment to begin. He had never really taken the time to look closely at her but, when he did, he was more aware of an unorthodox beauty that he felt she possessed. He had always pitied her circumstances but was more and more drawn to her fragility, her vulnerability, which he found troublingly attractive. Her meek, demure manner was in stark contrast to the abrupt and often fierce personality of Martha and Carlisle liked this. Despite his intentions to become closer to his wife he remained emotionally distant from her, especially since the birth of Peter. He hadn't wanted another child, but after the loss of Clara he felt obliged to provide Martha with the chance of another daughter. Not only did he detest any intention of 'replacing' Clara, but he also felt a palpable resentment that the new offspring was a boy.

He walked through a canopy of oak trees, on a gravel path next to a natural floodplain, pondering as he went as to how the rain, so often depressing for the human soul, nevertheless provided the nutrients for a rich soil in which livestock could graze. A small herd of Friesian cows, as if hearing his thoughts, peered up from their mechanical nibbling of the grass and low-standing celandine and stared directly at him as he passed. The transiency of life sung out: soon, those shiny kidney-shaped leaves would fade from yellow to white as the spring rolled into summer and another cycle would commence. A kingfisher stood proudly to his right, its sharp beak and orange plume radiant against its dark coat, watching intently as a pale, yellow brimstone butterfly danced playfully in front of it, almost aimlessly carried by the breeze, dreamily searching for buckthorn.

He crossed the small natural boundary – a low ditch that surrounded the river – which marked an entrance into Ruislip Court, where noisy workers replaced the animals, and the smell of hay, barley and grain replaced the drifting smell of the fauna. To his right stood the cow byre, containing a granary, and beside it the pig sties and stables. Already, there was a bustle of activity in the Great Barn, a large timber-framed building which served as the hub of the working day. Soon, the clattering of carts bringing various produce would drown out completely the cackling of the magpies and the cooing of the woodpigeons who viewed the activities from the safety of the many oak trees. Carlisle stopped opposite the Great Barn and viewed the remains of a Motte and Bailey castle. Very little remained of the fortress, except the earthen mound and the protective moat, which was now overgrown with blackberry bushes, docks, thistles and daisies. He tried to imagine the once-standing timber castle on top of the mound, built by the Norman settlers seven hundred years ago. It was not the panoptic design of Pentonville, he reflected, but the aim was the same: to watch closely the subordinate peasants and quickly intercept any signs of revolt or rebellion. Is it human nature to imprison, to control and, ultimately, to punish, he asked himself as he slowly walked on. Later, this entire 'Manor' would be owned by Kings College, Cambridge, who would maintain their watch from an intellectual distance.

A little way ahead stood the horse pond flanked by sleepy weeping willows, where the farm horses would drink and be washed. An old willow tree stood to his left, its trunk bent and distorted, choked by leaves, arched like a catapult in aim, ready to launch its adopted fledglings into the vicissitudes of life far away from the safety of their nest. The pond had a thin film of algae covering its surface in which the moorhens and coots would clean themselves and where in a couple of months the many three-spined sticklebacks would commence breeding, their throats and bellies turning red in the process. A fitting symbol, Carlisle reflected, for the poisonous fire afflicting his three parishioners.

Next to the pond stood Ansell's workshop and Carlisle could already smell the smoke from the furnace. Soon the sound of metal hammering on metal would be heard as the horses patiently became shod.

He turned his mind back to the task in hand. It was close to 8.00am, when they were to commence breakfast. He assumed and hoped that Ephraim would also be present to assist on this first morning when hostility and confusion were likely to greet him from the three cells. Indeed, before even reaching the entrance to St Martin's he heard a guttural, vulgar bellowing from Cell C, that of Henry Percivale. Carlisle inhaled deeply. The experiment had begun.

CHAPTER 7

Though your sins be as scarlet, they shall be as white as snow;
though they be like red crimson, they shall be as wool.
Isaiah 1:18

As it was the first day of the experiment, Carlisle had requested that all assembled in the church early. Being Ash Wednesday, he was expecting a larger than usual attendance at Communion and he wanted to begin before anyone else arrived.

"We stand here on the first day of Lent," he began, as Tom, Alice and Henry sat before him. "It is a day of renewed hope, which symbolises penance and forgiveness; a time for us all freely to admit our sins and seek earnestly to enter on a new path of righteousness. As the flowers in the graveyard are beginning to grow, so may we also flower into new creations."

The enthusiasm that Carlisle hoped would rub-off on his parishioners was sadly lacking as all three stared blankly at him.

"I ain't at school," said Henry sarcastically. "You wanna get my interest then 'ave a word 'bout the 'orses. Then I'm 'appy to listen. But flowers and graveyards, you can leave all that to the sexton over there," he said pointing to Ephraim and laughing. "That's his business."

"Mr Percivale," replied Carlisle, hoping that Ephraim would not take offence, "I do most respectfully ask that you embrace this opportunity for your sake and for Mr Ansell's. Most importantly, though, I urge you to embrace it for the sake of Christ."

At the mention of his employer, Percivale was reminded once more that his continued (and much-needed) employment was conditional upon his participation in this experiment. He therefore sat back with a grimace and chose to remain silent, only giving Ephraim a furtive glance.

"One of the traditional aspects of Lent," continued Carlisle, relieved that Percivale's sarcasm had been somewhat diminished, "is that such persons guilty of sins should openly declare their desire for penance to avoid the damnation of their souls. In so doing, they may also serve as a lesson for others who may then be afraid to sin themselves."

Carlisle was again met with silence.

"Therefore," he persevered, "in order that such discipline may be restored in you and enable you to take flight from such vices, it is suggested in here," he held up a small dark book, "that I read to you certain sentences from the Holy Book which, although bewailing such sinners as yourselves, will nevertheless set you on the path to earnest and true repentance."

Again, no-one spoke. Tom looked confused; Alice, terrified; Henry, fiercely angry.

"I therefore invite you," spoke Carlisle, looking back down at his book, "rather, I implore you, to respond with a simple 'Amen' to each of my declarations. I will indicate this with a gentle nod, as so," Carlisle continued, motioning accordingly with his head.

"Shall we commence?"

There was a murmur of confusion and discontent, so Carlisle

decided that the easiest way was for them to understand the ritual as they progressed. He therefore started the proceedings:

"Cursed is the man that maketh any carved or molten image, to worship it."

He nodded, expecting a response but was greeted with the familiar silence.

Carlisle smiled: "I remind you to answer with the word 'Amen' when I indicate to do so. Let us try that again."

This time the 'curse' was greeted with a rather robust 'Amen' from Tom, a gentle and quiet 'Amen' from Alice and what could only be described as a grunt from Henry.

"Splendid," said Carlisle, addressing them all, before continuing with the proceedings; Cursed is he that curseth his father or mother; that removeth his neighbour's land-mark; that maketh the blind to go out of his way; that perverteth the judgement of the stranger, the fatherless, and widow; that smiteth his neighbour secretly; that lieth with his neighbour's wife; that taketh reward to slay the innocent; that putteth his trust in man, and taketh man for his defence, and in his heart goeth from the Lord."

He paused before the final phrase, to catch his breath and imbue the conclusion with added significance.

"Cursed are the unmerciful, fornicators, and adulterers, covetous persons, idolaters, slanderers, drunkards, and extortioners."

The 'Amen' was said and Carlisle was surprised to find that he also joined in the conclusion. He closed his book and the proceedings.

Carlisle leaned back on his chair. It had been a long and demanding day and he was grateful to now be back to the relatively sanctuary of his study in the Vicarage. His thumb still showed the remnants of the ash he had imposed upon the foreheads of his parishioners after Communion. The day had, as anticipated, been wrought with difficulties as his three participants struggled with their new routine and Carlisle was not sorry when Percivale in particular departed for his daily employment with Ansell.

As well as their spiritual unease, their physical selves were also restless and unbalanced. Unused to a lack of alcohol even for a matter of hours, Tom's body had started a slow, silent scream for the poison that had flowed through him so often, so regularly and so destructively. He complained of a profound fear of life and 'horrible dread' in the pit of his stomach. This was accompanied, as so often when the drink was withdrawn, by feelings of guilt, shame and self-loathing. He slept on and off that first night, riddled with anxiety, his body and head entering various spasms and was subject to unusual, bewildering dreams. One such dream, which he later relayed to Carlisle, stayed in his mind. He had seen the dog before. Many times, in fact. But never this close, this wild, this intimidating. He could even smell its breath as it gnarled its teeth. He would run - he always did - but the faster he wanted to move the slower his legs would work. It happened all the time. He had to move, though. Run. He felt the dog behind him. He knew that it could easily pounce on him should it wish but it was evidently playing with him, toying with his fear. A small hall appeared into which he entered, sitting down on a creaky wooden seat. The dog didn't enter but he sensed it waiting outside. His teeth began to hurt. On the stage in the hall stood a man no more than three feet tall: an homunculus, laughing and spitting words. Tom registered the words without understanding them. From where or from whom did they originate? The homunculus disappeared, and the scene was now an unfamiliar garden. He was alone. No sign of the dog. It was cold. His teeth continued to hurt. A stream passed through the garden. He walked towards a tree, but the dog finally pounced before he reached it.

When back fully in the waking world, he had a growing feeling of nauseated panic when he realised that no alcohol would be coming his way for the next twelve hours, or the twelve hours after that. He was, of course, free to leave at any time, but where would he go? Lodging at *The George* did have its benefits: he would collect the empty (and not-so empty) glasses for Mr Clement *in lieu* of full rent and on several occasions had been forced off the premises after his urge for the drink had resulted in helping himself to whatever he could lay his hands on. He was aware that Mr Clement would not accept him back, the church was clearly not an option, and he was tired of sleeping in one of the many small ditches that surrounded the river.

At the same time, a weak, almost imperceptible light was growing inside him. He had for so long feared life and sought peace and refuge within the gin bottle or dregs of beer. Peace could only be found, he felt, by another administered dose of poison and so the viciously cruel cycle would continue unless he was physically forced, like now, to break the pattern. But he was realising the utter unmanageability of his life; his powerlessness over this poison and his need to rely on something other than Tom Morris.

Alice had spent her first day at the Vicarage, nervous and utterly in awe of Martha. After an hour or so of polite but firm instruction from her 'ma'am', as she called Martha, she had silently gone about her business of tending to Peter whilst Martha cooked; cleaned when and where directed and generally kept out of sight wherever possible. Carlisle had returned to the Vicarage in the afternoon and, from his study door, which he usually kept closed, had watched with fascination as Alice passed to and fro. For minutes he watched, unseen, as she looked tenderly over Peter while he slept in the room opposite, yet her eyes displaying evident sadness. The room in which Peter slept was neat, functional, with a bowl and can for washing. Next to the bed was a small table and Carlisle could just make out the copy of the children's Bible stories which he now read to Peter every evening. But his attention immediately returned to Alice. What was it about her that captivated him, Carlisle asked himself? What made him stop and voyeuristically peak through the door as she tended to his son?

He closed the door, breathing heavily. He silently prayed forgiveness and walked towards his desk. It was a good-sized room, flanked on all sides by rows of books and had the distinct look and smell of a university library. At Oxford, Carlisle had studied the traditional disciplines covering the classics and *Literae Humaniores*: rhetoric, moral philosophy, Latin, Euclidean geometry as well as the more specifically theological texts such as the Gospels (in Greek), Luther's Thirty-Nine Articles and Joseph Butler's *Analogy of Religion*. He remained deep, thorough but intellectually conservative in attitude, and whilst his peers were excitingly flirting with texts of the mystics like Swedenborg and Boehme, Carlisle was happy to retire for an evening accompanied by Tertullian or Augustine. The closest he had come to experimenting was with *The Spiritual Exercises*, although he found nothing within the text particularly offensive to his Protestant faith. On his desk stood a photo, that of his father, looking stern and starchy. To its left an inkwell and pen, several papers relating to parish affairs and research for his *History of St George's Chapel*. Leaning back on his chair he reached over to his desk drawer and removed his journal. Underneath he saw the diary that had been left to him a few months before and almost automatically he retrieved it and turned to the November 11 entry which still plagued him:

"Then, when they have had the Gospel drilled into their contorted skulls and shallow minds like sanctified trepanation and their desperate sinful state becomes a part of their very being like their dirty, stinking, prison uniform, open the pen-gate and toss them out into a new, unfamiliar pasture in which to graze on twigs and wallow in mud, preferably three-thousand miles away so the stench does not reach civilised England and corrupt the pure and holy incense of the Church. Heaven forbid! The glorious Church!"

He still could not understand the bitterness behind such a tirade. He had often felt that, like individuals, the Church should also confess its own sins but to whom? Who sat in authority on the Church except God Himself? Still puzzled, he placed the diary back in his drawer, opened his own journal and began to write.

March 1, 1843

I do not know what to expect from this experiment, but I must persevere. Ephraim has been of the utmost assistance and I will need him most definitely in the days and weeks to come. Percivale is a most disagreeable fellow and I have my doubts that he will remain for the duration of the allocated time. Such bitterness and hostility. There is a depth of anger in the man that I have rarely seen before. God knows that I must have patience with him, but his outburst at breakfast this morning, when he was most discourteous to Ephraim, troubled me. I will not speak with Ansell unless absolutely necessary, but I must take pains to make sure that he does not disrupt proceedings for Tom and Alice.

My heart continues to pity Tom and I sense a questioning soul underneath his physical decay. He posed some interesting questions following Communion, which I must admit I struggled to answer (why do I keep the chalice always to my right side? I had not previously given this a second's thought). He is suffering from lack of alcohol and was visibly shaking and sweating most profusely when I left him in his cell earlier (I will use the word 'cell' always to remind me of Pentonville and Harry Flynn). I will have recourse to call on Dr Trent should it be necessary, although I am assured that this is a normal reaction to the sudden extraction of the poison and should settle in a matter of days.

Alice commenced her domestic chores with Martha. She is such a meek child, somewhat lost and lonely, and I hope Martha is good to her (she can be so fierce, and I had to hold my tongue earlier). I will endeavour, as often as I can, to keep a close eye on her and ask Thomas to cover any of my duties should I be required here at the Vicarage. She is a *most fascinating creature and I feel I must protect her.*

It will prove impossible to follow 'The Spiritual Exercises' to the letter and that is not of initial concern. I must remind myself daily that it desires practical and imaginative prayer and meditation, not intellectual wisdom. Therefore, I will use what I feel is most expedient and discard that which may be beyond the grasp of them (neither Tom nor Henry seem able to read; Alice barely so).

Tomorrow I will commence early with the examen and choose accessible pages of Scripture on which they can all dwell and reflect. I will begin with Christ's baptism with Alice tomorrow. Nothing would give me greater pleasure than to baptise her into Our Lord's Church.

(Must write to Kingsmill re: Flynn. Peter: much crying again).

Carlisle retired to bed not long afterwards, but his thoughts rested on the three souls he held so precariously in his hands, as well as his own.

CHAPTER 8

"One, two, three…but where is the fourth?"
Plato, *Timaeus*

The following day saw a slight improvement in the weather and in Tom's physical health. There was, however, no improvement in Henry's mood: he yawned through Morning Prayer and scowled through Communion.

Tom remained in the pew at the end of the service as the other parishioners filed out. Carlisle noticed the thoughtful gaze on his face, which seemed fixed upon the large wooden crucifix behind the altar. Offering his brief farewells to the regular celebrants, Carlisle instructed Ragland to see Alice and Henry back to their cells. He paused momentarily to look at Alice and watch her reaction. She seemed placid yet nervous, as she most usually did, and Carlisle made a mental note to spend time with her later that morning discussing a passage of scripture.

Tom sat back, still looking at the wooden image on the wall. Such suffering, he felt. A faint smell of communion wine still hung in the air and he allowed his mind to wander. It left the church and went back to a time of his childhood. He saw himself in a dark room, much smaller than his current cell, and he could again smell the scent of wine. This time, however, there was also the odour of fear and faeces surrounding and clinging to him. The threatening voice of his father had subsided somewhat, placated after pounding the fragile body of his twelve-year-old son who now huddled in the corner of the room, terrified. Whatever had occurred to make his father beat him, it must be his fault, he reasoned in his immature mind. Why else would he be beaten? He must try harder, be better next time. If his father was angry then he must be suffering, so the warped reasoning continued, and if he is suffering then I must be the cause. He curled himself tightly again the wall of his room and wept with physical and emotional pain. His mother, now deceased, suddenly came into his mind: a saintly, devout woman who lived in constant fear of God and her husband and whose constitution had been defeated by the bitter winter of 1828.

Tom continued to let his mind wander. This time he was in an open field. He was drunk. He had seen his father drink from the clear glass bottle on many occasions and he wanted to be like his father. The liquid had burned his throat at first and then his courage. The field in which he now sat, a small pool of vomit in front of him, was located not far from their dwelling and where Tom often took himself away to be among the animals. This time, however, a huge, terrifying animal was also wishing to graze. An animal twice his size, carrying a birch rod and an anger that would have made even the Devil shudder. This animal was supposed to protect him, though? Make him feel safe? The logic failed again as the birch rod crashed against his back and his face was pushed viciously into the vomit. Must do better, he thought, when the animal finally left him alone. Must try harder. Must drink more. Must not vomit. Only children vomit, not real men. Such recollections made Tom shudder as though the pain was more severe than ever and brought him back to the present. His eyes were full of tears as he looked again at the wooden cross and tried to recall some of the words of Carlisle's recently finished sermon: "Whoever wants to be my disciple should take up his cross and follow me." His mind was still thick and heavy and unable to understand clearly. The words Carlisle used were too big for Tom; too laden with unintelligible meaning. As a child, and still now, Tom had always preferred images to words – clouds, trees, the moon - and so he continued to stare directly in front on him, reading the image of the crucifixion in his own visual way. An anger had slowly simmered within him though as he recalled his childhood reminiscences. His father had abandoned him and his mother not long after the incident in the field and was never to be seen or heard of again, but not before he had administered several other beatings. Tom had increasingly sought refuge in the bottle so that by the age of thirteen it was becoming a daily, stolen source of relief to his pain. But he was no longer a child, he thought to himself. Those days have now passed yet he remained trapped in his twelve or thirteen-year-old mind: not good enough; never good enough; the pain, anxiety and self-loathing are too much to bear, so obliterate it with intoxication and let the Devil alone care for the consequences.

He remained motionless, his eyes blinking from time to time, and a frown sitting heavily above them. Carlisle quietly moved up to him and sat down, relieved that Ragland's daily bucket of water had removed the smell of alcohol and urine as a disturbing chaperone. Tom felt Carlisle beside him and made a move to stand.

"Wait a little, Tom," spoke Carlisle, his eyes now also fixed upon the crucifix. It had been bequeathed by a recently departed parishioner and hung neatly on the wall. The subject's eyes looked painfully down to one side as though in sad recognition of its fate, a smattering of red oozed from his side. Soon, in keeping with the Lenten tradition, this statue, along with other crosses and images, would be veiled in violet cloth to prevent any other focus than that of Christ's work of Redemption. After the ceremonies on Good Friday, the crosses would be unveiled, and all the remaining images would follow likewise just before the Easter Vigil.

"You seem very interested in that statue," spoke Carlisle after a minute or so.

"Yes, sir," replied Tom. "I haven't really looked at it much before, but it makes me think for some reason. Not sure why. It's not a peaceful scene. Blood and everything. He looks in a good deal of pain, sir."

Carlisle nodded. "I imagine he was, Tom."

"But I still don't understand why he couldn't have just got off and walked away. You know, if he was God he could have just climbed down or pretended to be hurting when he really was not."

Tom immediately looked at Carlisle, worried about being irreverent. "I hope that's not bad to say, sir."

"Not at all," replied Carlisle. "One of the mysteries of the Christian faith is that Jesus was fully human as well as fully God. He suffered and felt pain just as we do. Indeed, this period of Lent is the perfect time for us to accept and embrace our suffering. It is –"

"– He can't be both, sir," Tom cut in quickly and rather sharply. "That makes no sense to me. Either you are a horse or a mouse. You can't be both. Makes my head hurt to think about him being both."

"We rely too much on our heads, Tom. Not enough on our

hearts," Carlisle replied, touching his breast somewhat dramatically.

"But if I can't understand it, sir, then I can't believe it. You can't be a horse and a mouse, I say again. Don't you think, sir?"

"I haven't really thought of it in those terms. But I think the lesson is that, in Christ, humanity and God are part of the same thing, unlike a horse and a mouse, which are two separate creatures." Carlisle felt uneasy with his lukewarm and illogical theology.

Tom frowned. "Still makes no sense to me, sir. I am not meaning to be rude but when I see that statue there I think of the mice that I used to catch in my room at Mr Clement's. They looked straight at me – right in the eye - and I think they knew they had no chance to escape, sir. Their pain was real. They were done for. But if Jesus was God, as you say he was, then he could've escaped. And if he couldn't have escaped then he can't be God." He paused as if trying to keep pace with his own logic. "Is that not right, sir? And if he couldn't have escaped, he must 'ave been right angry about the whole thing."

"It is one of the difficulties we have to face as Christians, Tom," replied Carlisle, unsure how to respond without drawing too deeply on his reserves of intellectual exposition. "If we rely too much on our minds we will try to understand things that are beyond us and get into all kinds of muddle."

"Muddle it is, sir," said Tom. "It all goes around in my head and makes me feel quite dizzy. And all that chatter about the wine becoming blood. Makes no sense at all to me. No sense at all." Carlisle remained silent, lost on how to proceed.

"You want me back in my cell now, sir?" asked Tom suddenly and rather despondently as he recalled his dark, childhood room that had caused him so much pain.

"Yes," answered Carlisle, somewhat absent-mindedly, "I will be with you shortly and we can continue this discussion if you wish."

"As you please, sir," replied Tom, rising slowly with one further look at the crucifix. He shook his head slightly. "You can't be a horse and a mouse," he muttered again to himself as he walked slowly towards the church door.

Carlisle made little progress with Tom that morning. It was bitterly cold in the cell and Tom wrapped the thin blanket around him as Carlisle spoke rather monotonously about the rite of the Communion. Tom looked sad, distant and after twenty minutes or so Carlisle felt it more appropriate to leave him to his solitary confinement. As for Tom, he lay on his makeshift bed and withdrew a small, blunt pocket knife from his trouser pocket. He turned his head to the temporary partition that separated his cell from the next and began to scratch slowly into the wood.

Carlisle felt uncomfortably glad that he was now able to visit Alice, who resided in the neighbouring cell. The intimacy provided by the small space tugged on Carlisle's heart a little as he sat on the rickety stool in her room whilst she perched on the edge of the makeshift bed. She looked pale, but alert. Her hair had been tamely washed with the soap that rested in a congealed puddle on her table and tried feebly to dance over her rakish shoulders. Her face was now largely clear from the bruising that had been meted out to her before she arrived, and her thin lips offered a half-smile. Alice broke the uncomfortable silence.

"I have been thinking a good deal about the baptism story you told me yesterday," she began.

"That's good, Alice," replied Carlisle eagerly. "Please, share your thoughts."

Alice paused. All throughout her young life she never felt that she had the permission to speak her own thoughts. She had not known her real father: he had died shortly before she was born, and her mother had re-married soon afterwards. Her step-father had reminded her on many occasions that she wasn't really 'his' and so she preferred either to agree with him or remain silent. There was little love or religious faith in her life growing up and now she was faced with Carlisle asking her opinion on something so profound.

"Alice?" prompted Carlisle as the silence ensured.

Composing herself, almost holding her breath, Alice spoke softly and slowly.

"You see, I have tried my best, honest I have, to do what you suggested and imagine Jesus having his baptism. You know, going under the water and feeling it with my eyes and ears but I can only go a little way before I have to stop. It scares me." Carlisle remained silent. Alice continued.

"I used to be put under the water quite often, you see. But not nicely as with Jesus in a river. No, it wasn't nice."

She looked down to one side, evidently recalling something of intense pain.

"All the water went into my ears. I can still hear it now," she continued, lifting her frail hands as if in protection from an unseen foe. "Then, depending how long I was under the water, and my breath couldn't hold out no more, then it would all go in mouth too, and my eyes. It wasn't nice water neither, not like the water Jesus went into. Horrible water it was. Dirty, filthy water. Carlisle leaned forward slightly. "What are you describing to me, Alice?"

But it was as though Alice was a world away and had entered back into the time she was describing.

"I can remember," she continued, "that after a little while it was as though time stopped completely. Even that sound was no longer in my ears and I couldn't feel nothing. It felt nice then. Peaceful. I would have stayed in that feeling if I could have. But I would always feel the big hand grab my hair and pull my face out and my senses would all come rushing back to me at once. And that face with the big hand would be staring at me, laughing."

She paused, as though emerging from her painful reverie, and looked at Carlisle.

"Jesus saw a dove when he came out the water; I saw a horrible face."

She paused again.

"That's why I prefer to call God 'Love'. Nothing else. Not 'Father', 'Master', 'Lord', 'Him' - just 'Love'."

CHAPTER 9

As a dog returns to its vomit, so a fool repeats his folly
Proverbs 26:11

March 2, 1843
Tom relayed to me his dream about a dog, which he believed was pursuing him. I can only conclude that this is a natural symbol for his predicament with the drink that seeks to capture and destroy him. He seemed extremely agitated this morning as a result and complained of a searing thirst. I attempted to work on my 'St George's', but I fear this month will leave me little time for anything other than this experiment. For the first week, I must allow all three to grow used to their new surroundings before we explore more deeply their sins and vices.

March 5, 1843
Tom appears in better physical condition with every day and his comments on the rite of Communion and certain passages of Scripture continue to fascinate me (why are there only three members of the Holy Trinity, like a triangle and not four, like a square?). I returned home at lunch, much to Martha's evident dismay (why?), to keep a watchful eye on Alice. She is so tender and gentle with Peter

and has a surprising intellect, which is very far removed from her rather bedraggled look. I feel a strong sense of care towards her. I will instruct Ephraim to provide her with extra soup and bread as she is a frail creature and deserves to feel loved. I engaged briefly with Henry before his departure to Ansell. He gives little thought to the 'Exercises' or Scriptural exposition. I had my first dream of dear Clara for some weeks. It left me somewhat disturbed when I awoke.

March 7, 1843
I have started to deepen the 'Exercises', beginning with an acceptance of their sins and a need for repentance. Little progress with Percivale. Tom seems more willing to engage and I feel a genuine desire for change within him. He spoke today, most earnestly, of 'surrender.' Alice briefly relayed her troubled history, with which I was not familiar, and it is has only served to make me think more affectionately, almost lovingly, of her. I managed a brief hour on 'St George's.'

March 9, 1843
A most disturbing dream. A dog (Tom's?) sat on my knees, black in colour, and proceeded to lick my neck. Most unpleasant. I feared it would bite me, but rather it kissed me! What it could mean is beyond me. Wrote to Kingsmill today at Pentonville. Relayed how splendidly things were going here and requested information concerning

Flynn. I am most keen to compare how the separate system works for him and for Tom.

March 11, 1843
I dreamed that a young boy had run off with my white shirt, leaving me quite naked. I was barefoot and took to my heels after him. I cannot recall whether or not I caught him and remain equally unsure as to what the dream could mean. I am quite certain, though, that Clara was involved. It pains me to feel her presence, yet to be unable to understand the meaning of such feelings. Alice and Martha spoke at length today. I could not hear what they were discussing. Alice seems anxious but continues to care for Peter in a very tender way and I am tempted to increase her hours here at the Vicarage.

March 13, 1843
I had a strange feeling today as I entered church. It was as if someone was watching me. The church was empty, however. Nevertheless, the feeling was strong. A foreboding? I sat with Clara for some time afterwards. How dreadfully I miss her. I have little appetite, much to Martha's consternation. I noticed that Tom is carving an image into the wood of one of his walls. I cannot, as yet, make out what the image is. I will ask Tom.

It was overcast, and the Vicarage was bathed in a rather gloomy light. Martha sat in a small room next to the parlour. To her left, the narrow back staircases hung winding from the attic to the kitchen. Beside her, also seated, was the frail-looking Alice. Her head was bowed, evidently crying.

"Alice, tell me again what happened," asked Martha, leaning forward so as to try and catch her eyes.

Alice held her breath for what seemed a long time and slowly raised her head. "I was just walking here as normal, ma'am, and by the pump at *The George* a rat ran out in front of me. As big as me, it was. This big," she held both hands in front her to indicate the size. "It ran across the path and then straight back again like it was lost and wanted to run back to its hole, but a cart was coming and ran right over it. The noise was horrible, but it was stone dead and the cart just went on its way. I couldn't bear myself to look at the dead rat with all that blood."

She paused, evidently distressed. "Sorry for saying so, ma'am. It's just got me all flustered, that's all."

Martha smiled compassionately and placed an arm around Alice.

"Firstly, you must stop calling me ma'am but rather Martha."

"I prefer ma'am, if you don't mind. It sounds more proper,"

"As you wish," Martha smiled again. "Now, tell me what has been happening at the almshouses with Reverend Carlisle. I have tried to leave things be as best I can. Has anything there upset you?"
"Reverend Carlisle has been very kind, ma'am. Very kind," Alice replied, still trying to compose herself, "but this experiment

thing has got me thinking a great deal and not all of it is pleasant memories, if you understand."

Martha placed her arm a little more tightly around Alice's shoulder.

"Tell me, Alice," she said. "Tell me what is unpleasant."

Alice closed her eyes, as if the memory of the rat were now being replaced by another, deeper and more disturbing vermin. She breathed deeply and relayed to Martha her bitter experiences in the bath tub with her step-father.

Once she had finished, she was both surprised and embarrassed to find her cheeks further wet with tears. Martha looked at her tenderly, her arm still around the young shoulders.

"You have been very brave in telling me all this, Alice," said Martha, "And I think I understand what has happened."

Alice looked up at Martha, her eyes still glistening.

"You do, ma'am?" she asked timidly.

Martha smiled more obviously and turned to face Alice.

"I do," she said. "Let me explain. We are often given symbols and signs, every day of our lives, but we rarely see or understand them. We think only of ourselves and our own business, sadly." Alice continued to look into Martha's eyes, which had reassuring warmth.

"You see," she continued, "sometimes when we are in need or in spiritual trouble we dream these signs and symbols. They are there to help us. And sometimes, when the soul is in particular distress, these symbols break out of our dreams and into our real lives."

Alice frowned. "Forgive me, ma'am," she said, "but I'm not too good with clever things like this."

Martha smiled again. "Then let me put it more simply. The rat you saw was a symbol - a symbol of the dirtiness, the filth, the disease that you see inside yourself."

Alice shuddered a little at the strength of these words. "But I didn't dream it, ma'am. It will be there on the path now. Lying there."

"I know you didn't dream it," Martha continued. "Many people do dream about horrible things like rats, but they remain just that – dreams, which then get hidden inside us again. The soul of most people is not yet ready to confront their inner self with their own eyes."

Alice frowned again, obviously and entirely perplexed.
"But your soul was ready, Alice, and the rat broke through from your dream into your waking day. Your soul wanted to show you something wonderful, something that you could see with your own eyes."

"See what, ma'am?"

Martha began after a short pause, "My mother once told me, when she was going through a very troubling period, that she dreamed night after night about a large black crow. The crow would even rest at the foot of her bed during the dream. Caw, caw, caw, it went."

Alice looked terrified, but Martha continued.

"Until one day my mother realised what it was that troubled her so. She never told me what exactly, and I never asked, but one day, as wide awake as can be, she saw the very same crow of her dreams as she was out in the fields. The crow looked at her, my mother looked back and then the bird took off on the wind, straight ahead, up and away and disappeared. My mother told me that after that she never once dreamed of the crow again and, whatever the problem was, her soul was eased."

Alice remained silent at first and then tentatively spoke: "Forgive me again, ma'am, but I am unsure what this means for me."

"It means that your rat is now dead," said Martha with a sudden passion in her voice. "It can no longer harm you or upset you."

Alice looked at her, still unsure of what to say but silently imploring her to carry on.

"It means that the filth and the dirtiness that you saw within you are now also dead," Martha continued. "By confronting your experiences as a child for the first time, however painful they may be, you have also defeated them. You remember what you told me: the rat had nowhere to run, nowhere to hide. As with my mother's experience, the crow was no longer welcome and so took flight. As bitter as it was, and as foul as it smelt, you have had your baptism, my dear child - your true baptism, but it is only now that you can see it." She threw both arms around a bewildered Alice.

March 16, 1843

Much progress made with the 'Exercises' today, as we imagined the Lord at twelve years of age remaining in the Temple. I had given little thought to my own childhood in Edinburgh, but I do recall my fear and anxiety. I assume this coincided with changing schools from George Herriot's to Royal High School. Twelve years is a most tender age and I do not recall it fondly. Both Tom and Alice seemed hesitant to share their own experiences of that time of their lives, but I encouraged them to try. Percivale said little but seemed to listen with an unusual interest.

March 17, 1843

Martha and Alice were again engaged in deep conversation today, which stopped as soon as I arrived. I can only assume that they were talking about me. Alice seems less anxious, more content and, dare I say, happier? I dreamed of Clara again. I am seeking solace next to her more and more. I removed more of the creeping ivy from Lucy's grave. I must ask Ephraim to tend to this more carefully.

March 19, 1843

Tom informed me this morning that the image that he has been scratching into the wood of his cell is of himself. There is little artistic talent to the image, yet it seems a most vicious face. He said, most interestingly, that the image provides him with solace when, as soon as he leaves his cell for Communion, he walks straight into the 'death of the churchyard.' He believes he has been in 'prison' all of his life. Quite a profound thought. Today being the Solemnity of St Joseph, I ask myself, as I often do, what will become of Peter? Alice seems very close to Martha and I witnessed Martha embrace her, something I have longed to do myself. A positive change seems to have come over Alice; I cannot fathom any other reason for this than my continued help with the 'Exercises'. This gladdens my heart.

CHAPTER 10

Is anyone among you suffering, let him pray. Is anyone cheerful?
Let him sing psalms.
James 5:13

Reverend Joseph Kingsmill
Chaplain
HMP Pentonville
Caledonian Road
London
March 20th, 1843

Reverend Edwin Carlisle, M.A. Oxon
St Martin's Church Vicarage
Borough of Middlesex

My esteemed Reverend Carlisle,
*   I continue to thank you for your correspondence and information concerning your experiment. It occurs to me that a great deal can be learned from your methods and approaches to solitary confinement and the problems of intoxication. Alas, it appears that such lessons have not been heeded here and thus it is with much dismay that I must inform you of the death of Mr Harry Flynn some two days ago. It was felt that his mental and spiritual constitution had improved somewhat following consultations with Dr Samuels but evidently this was not so. I will spare you the details, suffice to say that the deceased was found by one of the officers in the morning of Monday during routine inspection. The means of death was asphyxiation and his body has been removed*

to the prison morgue. His soul will, I pray, now rest with the Lord. I cannot, as is natural, help but ask myself if there was not more that I could have done to help in this case. Reverend Ralph apportions no blame, of course, but I have slept poorly these last couple of nights. Could we have seen this earlier? Rather, could I have seen this earlier? It is with pain that I can neither answer that question nor offer a solution. Only the day before this tragedy he had written to his father, but the letter remained unsent and was found inside his Bible. I reproduce it for you now with a heavy heart:

"Dear Father, Oh! How often do I wish I had never been born, to have brought so much disgrace upon such a kind father! but I hope you freely forgive me. Oh! that I could comfort you in your old age, instead of being a burden! I know, my dear father, that you have shed many tears, and uttered many sighs, on my account. How many hours do I keep awake, and fancy that I hear your voice speaking, and telling me to keep from bad company, or it would be the ruin of me. If I had done this, it would have been different with me at the present, but it is too late now. I hope it is not too late to be forgiven for all my wickedness. I pray to God morning, noon and night, to give me a new heart, instead of this wicked one that I have got."

If anything good can come of such an event, it will, I have no doubt. As I write, Lord Wharncliffe has called an immediate meeting of the prison commissioners and explicitly requested the attendance of Reverend Ralph. I am unsure as to what the outcome will be, and I will endeavour to keep you abreast of all developments. The funeral of Mr Flynn will be conducted by Reverend Ralph on the morning of this coming Monday. Mr Flynn's kin have naturally been informed: his father is unwell and unable to travel but his sister has already made herself present at the prison morgue. There is evident anger and hostility from them towards us all.

Forgive me, dear Reverend, if I close this brief letter on such a painful note but duties require me to serve the Lord in this sad event.

I have the honour to remain,
Yours in Christ,
Joseph Kingsmill

March 24, 1843

I awoke with a most severe headache after little sleep. I have little inclination to write today. I still have little appetite. In truth, I have little appetite for anything. Alice gives me scant attention. Her mind appears occupied elsewhere.

March 27, 1843

The letter from Kingsmill concerning the death of Harry Flynn has left me out of sorts all day. Why has Flynn succumbed to despair under separate confinement, yet Tom has flourished? Naturally, conditions and timescales are very different, yet Tom has kept rigorously to his schedule, remaining in his cell for the allocated time. I was under the impression from Kingsmill that Flynn had started off life in Pentonville in a positive manner. What changed? Could it have been Ralph's fierce proselytising from the first day he entered his cell? I have endeavoured to let Tom find his own direction and embrace the imaginative side of the 'Exercises'. I cannot but think that such an approach would have been sanctioned most *vehemently by Ralph. Tom has evidently benefitted most considerably from his own understanding of God, whom, like Alice, he now simply calls 'Love'. Could it be that Tom was ready to change – to surrender – and Flynn was not? If this is so, then Tom's change would have happened regardless of the confinement to which he has been subject, as has happened also with Alice, who has considerably more freedom outside of her cell than has Tom. No, separate confinement is not the victor in Tom's case. Separate confinement has only been victorious with the poor demise of Harry Flynn.*

Upon receiving Kingsmill's letter, I felt a strong, inner desire to see Alice and share the news with her. But why? She knew Flynn not at all. I relayed this inclination to Ephraim, who chastised me for such thoughts. I went to see Clara instead and spoke with her for some time. I am convinced she has something to tell me. Henry appeared intoxicated again today and I have no option but to inform Ansell on the morrow. I will not be sad to see the back of him. My thoughts constantly return to Flynn (and Alice). I suffered a further headache and was forced to rest in the study for the best part of an hour.

It was a bright but cold morning and Carlisle was surprised when Henry stopped him as he was leaving his cell.

"I want to go to confession. Tomorrow," Henry immediately

requested, with an unusual mischievousness. "You talk on and on about it every morning and so I will do it."

Carlisle hesitated. Henry had not previously expressed any interest in engaging with scripture, prayer or any element of spiritual guidance.

"By all means, Henry," said Carlisle, feigning genuine concern. "Is there anything specific you wish to confess?"

"I'll tell you tomorrow," Henry answered, his eyes now cold. "You say it is private. Just me and you?"

"And God, of course," answered Carlisle. "But yes, anything that you declare in confession will remain unknown to others. It is a chance to clear the soul of anything that is an obstacle to our relationship with Christ."

"Good," replied Henry, still coldly. "Tomorrow then. I'll be off to Mr Ansell's now."

Carlisle watched Henry leave the churchyard, his large gait swaying a little as he walked. Thoughtfully, he walked towards Alice's cell and paused by the door. He knew she would be inside as it was not yet time for her to leave for the Vicarage. His heart beat faster and he would have knocked were it not for a call from Ragland who was standing outside the church door.

Ephraim had always, where possible, avoided confrontation and his heart burned with dismay as he left the church and slowly walked back to his lodgings at *The George*. He stopped in front of the pump to wash his hands, cleanse his worried soul and recalled the conversation that had just taken place. He had been unsure about the merits of this experiment from the outset and was growing increasingly concerned about Carlisle's own mental state, let alone those of the 'prisoners.'

"She's no more than a child, sir. And a very scared one," he had said to Carlisle as he saw him pause by her door. "Forgive me for saying so, sir," he had continued, "but I think Mrs Carlisle is the better one to care for her rather than yourself."

This had riled Carlisle and his temper betrayed the feelings that the young girl had formed within him.

"I would do well to remind you of your duties, Ephraim," Carlisle had replied in an unusually hostile tone, "and keep any advice to yourself."

"I am only remembering the situation with Miss Lucy a couple of years ago, sir, before she fell ill. That's all."

Carlisle was shocked. "I was merely supporting Lucy Sherwood in a time of need. I see no parallels whatsoever with this situation."

"All I am saying, sir, is that I worry you are developing the same feelings of affection for Miss Alice as you did for Miss Lucy. I wouldn't think that to be a good thing, just as the drink isn't a good thing for any of them" he nodded towards the almshouses. "I am not sure there's a great deal of difference between you all, sir."

"What in Heaven's name is your meaning?" asked Carlisle.

"Well, sir, if I am honest, once certain feelings get a hold of you, as when drink gets inside of them, I fear you're done for."

Carlisle exploded, his voice raised with bitterness: "My duties for Lucy were purely ministerial towards a young woman in need. The time I spent with her was of necessity. After the one regrettable instance of tenderness we shared, and which Lucy most inexplicably relayed to you, I immediately sought God's forgiveness at once."

"As I told you most honestly at the time, sir, the confession of Miss Lucy to me will never be heard by another soul, of that I can assure you."

"As well it should not be," continued Carlisle, still with his voice raised and breath heavy. "And as vicar of this church I have every right to administer love and tenderness to whomever I choose and when I wish. And if I now wish to protect Alice and demand that you provide her with extra soup and bread then I will do just that." He paused, regained his composure and concluded: "I hope I have made myself perfectly clear, Ragland." Ephraim was taken aback and hurt by Carlisle's unfamiliar use of his surname but before he could make any reply, a noise caused them both to turn. No more than ten metres behind them stood the grinning face of Henry Percivale.

Carlisle froze, his anger suddenly abandoning him.

"You should be at Mr Ansell's by now," he spoke, with an evident tremor in his voice. "What brings you back here?"

"This does," said Percivale still grinning and holding up a small blacksmith's knife. "I left it in my room. Can't shoe a horse without it!"

"I see," replied Carlisle, still rather flustered and a little lost for words.

Percivale placed the knife back in his pocket and slowly walked past the vicar and his sexton. Carlisle caught the unmistakable smell of alcohol. When he had walked no more than five metres Percivale stopped and turned his head.

"Confession tomorrow, remember, Reverend? Confession tomorrow," he had spoken with evident glee before making his way along the path and out of the churchyard.

March 28, 1843
Percivale's unexpected return during my conversation with Ephraim about Alice and Lucy has played exceedingly on my mind. What, exactly, did he hear? I found it impossible to concentrate on any other duties all day.

CHAPTER 11

Why were you searching for me? Were you not aware that I had to be in my Father's house?
Luke 2:49

Henry sat upright opposite Carlisle. Communion had ended, and they were alone.

"Just you and me," began Henry, a familiar smell of alcohol issuing from his breath.

"And God," replied Carlisle, "as I mentioned yesterday." He was apprehensive about what may be coming but he maintained a posture of authority as best he could.

"It's a nice church you got here, Reverend," began Percivale, looking around him. "Plenty of silver 'n' stuff, poking out from behind those cloths. Must be worth a pretty penny."

"Was there something you wanted to confess, Henry?" said Carlisle, unwilling to be drawn into superfluous conversation.

"Well, since you ask," replied Henry leaning back, "you know how you got us to do all those exercise things. The Bible things. Well, if I'm 'onest I don't really give tuppence about the Bible and all that, but one exercise we did got me thinking."

"And which exercise was that?" asked Carlisle.
"When you told us to think about Jesus as a twelve-year-old. You know, when he went missing. Parents couldn't find him 'ere nor

there."

"When they found him in the Temple, yes."

"Not much we know about the boy, is there?"

"The Gospels focus more on his adult ministry, when he –"

"– but you told us to imagine him as a twelve-year-old. So I did. And you know what I thought?"

Carlisle immediately again recalled his own time as twelve-year-old in Edinburgh: the privileged son of the eminent Charles Carlisle M.D, with any paternal disrespect or disobedience quite out of the question. "Tell me," he demanded quietly.

"I thought of Jesus being where I was when I was a lad," continued Henry.

"And where was that?" replied Carlisle, somewhat confused.

"Bridewell Prison. That's where. Two years of it. Not sure if they 'ad prison where Jesus was or he might 'ave ended there too. You know, disobeying his parents. That's just what I did."

"I am sorry to hear that, Henry. Is this what you wished to confess to me?"

Henry went on, ignoring Carlisle's question.

"You see, I was twelve once. Scrawny little urchin, really. Nothing but skin and bones," he looked surprised as he placed his hands over his now evident paunch.

Carlisle remained silent.

"My Pa did his best for us – me and me sisters. Used to work in the fields but you see the pennies were hard to come by and so he turned to bad things. 'Corse, I had no understanding at first. Did what he wanted. He was my Pa. Not for me to ask any questions of my Pa, is it?"

"Please continue," Carlisle responded.

"There was a small wooden outhouse he had built himself close to the room we all lived in. Six of us in that room. Smelt worse than Ansell's horses. I used to be 'appy to get out. Smell better air, you know. Six of you in one small room ain't no fun."

"I can quite understand that, Henry," Carlisle replied. "Was there something about the room that frightened you?"

Henry laughed a little. "Weren't *that* room that got my skin all crawly," he said, instinctively rubbing both his forearms. "But the other little room outside."

Carlisle frowned but remain silent.

"You see," continued Percivale, "my Pa couldn't get no pennies just working in the fields, so he started collecting little things to sell."

"That sounds a very common and sensible move. Many need to do whatever it takes to –"

"Children," cut in Percivale. "That's what he was selling. Boys and girls."

Carlisle stopped at once, unable to reply.

"Small boys and girls. Kept them in that little room outside. We was told to keep right away from them. Made a din they did though. Cry, cry, cry morning and night. Made me 'ead sore with the noise, it did."

He shuffled a little in his seat, wiped his nose with the cuff of his sleeve, and continued.

"One time the din was so bad I couldn't 'elp myself. Being twelve years, you know, and the only fella to my sisters, I wanted to put an end to that din, so I took myself to that room outside."

He looked at Carlisle, who remained motionless.

"Stunk to heaven it did. Worse than inside. There was one little girl there, all mess down her legs. 'Orrible smell. She was the one making the din. On and on and on, she went. She would have woken me sisters if she 'ad gone on like that. Cry, cry, cry."

Carlisle managed to speak. "And what was your response?"

"Smashed 'er on the 'ead with a pipe, I did. Like this." He brought his right hand down onto his leg with considerable force. "Pap, Pap, Pap. She stopped the din then alright."

"You killed her?" asked Carlisle, trying to remain calm but clearly struggling.

"Didn't know at the time, did I," answered Percivale. "Was only twelve, I tell you. But I knew summin' weren't right, so I took 'er out the room. Blood everywhere and all that. Got all her mess on me too from carrying her. Was gonna dump her in the field close by. Leave her there."

"And did you?" Carlisle asked, his voice increasing with anger.

"Didn't 'ave the chance, did I? Got seen by some constable walking around with his lamp. Didn't know what to do. Dropped the girl but he weren't 'aving none of it and grabbed my arms real tight. Was taken down the station. Never saw me sisters or Pa again. Two years in Bridewell Prison. Got off pretty lightly, I think."

He stopped. Carlisle remained seated, but his face was flushed with anger.

"Bet that didn't 'appen to your Jesus when he was twelve, did it?" Percivale said, with a faint smile.

"Why are you telling me this, Henry?" asked Carlisle as calmly as he could.

"Confession, ain't it," came Percivale's curt reply, again wiping his nose on his cuff. "That's what you tell us every morning. Confess your sins or you'll be burned up in Hell. Well that's what I am doing."

"But this happened, I imagine, twenty years ago?" cut in Carlisle.

"Why now?"

"Let me tell you why now, shall I?"

Carlisle didn't reply but offered a small nod of his head.

"When I got out of Bridewell, didn't have nowhere to go. Did try to go back to where we was before but they'd upped and gone. I think my Pa didn't fancy me dropping him in the clink, too. So I did this and that. Was fourteen or so and had picked up some good tips in Bridewell so I got by. Ended up working on a farm, don't know quite where. Was there a year or two, moved around and ended up here, with Ansell."

Carlisle was puzzled by the direction of the narrative but Percivale continued.

"You know young Stanley Hawkins? Works with me at Ansell's," asked Henry, suddenly.

"He is the apprentice blacksmith? Yes, I know who you mean."

"He's under my charge, is Hawkins. Will do anything I say. Meek as a lamb. I have ten years' age on him, you see."

"Henry, I am struggling to follow how this is all relevant to why you are telling me your dreadful story now."

"Well, you see, first night that Hawkins got his pay – not much of it, mind – I told 'im it would be good for 'im to give me a little drink. That's 'ow it goes in the business. So I takes 'im to *The Swan* and within no time 'is 'ead is swimming in the beer. Funny to see, it was. Quiet lad but given the beer he started talking and cackling like a magpie. And that's when he told me."

"Told you what, exactly?" asked Carlisle.

"Told me that before coming up 'ere, you know, to Ruislip, he worked with a family back in the city and guess who was there."

Carlisle shook his head. "I would not have any idea."

"Your sexton!" laughed Percivale. "Ephraim Ragland!"

Carlisle processed all that was being said and tried to find the connection.

"That is a nice coincidence of fate."

"Call it what you want, Reverend. But fate don't interest me.

What does though is what Ragland told Hawkings some years back and which then Hawkings told me."

A chill began to run through Carlisle's angular figure as he recalled the desperate moment in the empty almshouse where Ephraim had relayed his past. He found it impossible to speak.

"That Ragland had a young girl. Don't remember 'er name. From the same part of the city I was as a boy."

Carlisle remained frozen to the spot. Percivale continued.

"Was never good with numbers and that but I reckon the timings work out right. You know, the time when I did what I did."

Carlisle's hands were now shaking as his raised a long, thin finger. "Don't say another word, Percivale," he croaked, any Christian charity with which he may have received this confession had all but left him. "Not one more word."

Percivale noted the coldness and hostility in Carlisle's voice and demeanour.

"But I am confessing," he spoke, "confessing all my horrible and dirty sins so that I can become as white as snow. Ain't that what you say every morning? Ain't it?" he now also was beginning to rage a little. "We can't all be as perfect as your little twelve-year-old Jesus now, can we?"

Carlisle's own rage had now intensified. He tried to close his eyes, pray for patience and pity, but Percivale made that impossible.

"I ain't too proud of what I done," he said. "But it is what it is. Anyway, she was only a tiny girl. Covered in mess and cry, cry, cry. Not much of a loss."

"Get out," repeated Carlisle rising from his chair.

"I don't think that is very Christian of you, Reverend," Percivale said as he duly rose.

"Get out, Percivale," repeated Carlisle.

"I'll be getting out then," smiled Henry, arrogantly. "'Ave no fear of that. I'm a miserable sinner, remember. As you keep reminding me. Will leave you to your young ladies. You seem to like them from what you and the sexton were saying yesterday."

"There are sinners," roared Carlisle once more, now standing upright, crimson in the face "and there are *impertinent* sinners. Now, GET OUT, I TELL YOU!"

CHAPTER 12

My God, my God, why have You forsaken me?
Mark 15:34

March 29, 1843
Disturbing dream, the details of which I cannot fully recall this morning. Yet I know Clara was present. I am still in shock at Percivale's confession yesterday. His drunken outburst during Communion this morning, when he shouted out my conversation with Ephraim about my feelings for Lucy and Alice, has left me weak and feverish. Was it to punish me for my reaction to his confession? He had the audacity to tell me to check my eye for a plank, leaning drunk against a column in the nave. I do not know where to turn. Alice has said nothing and is concentrating solely on her domestic chores for Martha. I believe I caught her looking at me earlier today, almost in sympathy, though it was but a passing glance as I left the Vicarage. I have no knowledge as to Martha's thoughts and I have not the courage to ask. I pray that she puts Percivale's outburst down to no more than the incoherent ramblings of a drunkard. But I fear all is lost. Dear Clara, save me.

March 30, 1843
I must, at all costs, keep my faculties together this

morning. Alice must not know of my sleepless night. I must continue to function to the very best of my abilities, though my heart is heavy and ready to burst. Martha has said little to me since Tuesday and I know she is pained by the gossip-mongers relaying the outburst of Percivale. I feel done for and so utterly alone. Is my reputation beyond repair? Time will tell but the only time I have in front of me now is this morning's Communion. I can sense the eyes of disgust looking upon me already. Lord, have mercy on me, a sinner. Free me from the snare of the hunters.

Carlisle closed his Journal. The morning was bright and warm, but he shivered as he struggled to raise himself from his chair. He felt a profound need to spend time again next to the grave of Clara before Communion and imagine her playing with Elizabeth in heaven.

Upon arriving at the church, he headed immediately for the vestry. He turned and looked behind him twice, convinced that he was being watched. He saw nothing and no one. He took the chalice and pall, ciborium for the bread, corporal cloth and purificator to cleanse the chalice after use from the safe in the vestry and placed these on a small table behind the altar, next to a large black service book. But he was already trembling and struggling to hold the chalice and the candles as he lighted them. He paused and tried to catch his rapid breath. He managed to place the flagons with water and wine on the altar and returned to the vestry, where he sat down gratefully, relieved that no sermon was required today.

He could hear the church door open and a smattering of feet indicated the arrival of some of the congregation. He was further thankful that, being a weekday, the attendance would be small and so did not require assistance from his curate. He wiped his forehead again and tried to pray but his mind was drowning with the words of the upcoming Communion: *...examine thyself...lest you eat and drink your own damnation...*

It was time. He struggled to his feet, left the vestry and slowly walked into the church, down the nave flanked by the octagonal columns. He reached the altar in a state of dizziness, as if roaring waters were buffeting his mind, to and fro, and used the large wooden chair to steady himself. He lifted the chalice and his eyes – bloodshot, sinful, terrified – reflected straight back from the smudged silver vessel as if they had nowhere else to go, nowhere else to hide.

He placed the chalice back down in front of him, to the left. His hand shook. Removing his handkerchief, he again slowly wiped his brow and faced his small congregation. The uncomfortable feeling of omnipotence that he had first experienced at Pentonville pervaded him again and he looked from side to side. Something was making him feel terribly uneasy. Unlike on Sundays, when he stood at the pulpit in the centre of the church and could view everyone present, now he stood slightly to the right of centre, behind the altar. He was not in control. He had experienced this feeling of unease more and more over the last month: the feeling that it was not he that was doing the teaching or the admonishing or judging but Someone Else. Someone was watching *him.* He was the object of someone else's gaze; someone older and more powerful than he; someone who silently watched him every time he entered the church; someone stronger than even the collective eyes of the congregation.

He paused and wiped his brow again. Tom was in his familiar position in the pew, towards the end of the church. Henry was nowhere to be seen. Ephraim sat a few rows back to his right, a look of concern on his face. Alice sat in an accustomed position next to Martha, who held Peter on her knee as he struggled to free himself from his mother's arms. A small, bronze statue of St Martin, silhouetted against a candle, kept a close eye on Carlisle as he struggled to find the words to say the blessing and conclude the Communion.

And then he saw it. He saw what had been watching him; what had been judging him, admonishing him. He shuddered with the realisation. Opposite the faint prison bars etched into the wall, to the left of where he had stood every day for the last month, and almost for the last eight years, two eyes bored into him, aflame: they were the eyes of Pride that sat on its throne as it was attacked by the skeletal figure of Death: Pride, the chief of the Seven Deadly Sins, as he had himself taught Ephraim. He now realised that this experiment had nothing to do with Pentonville; nothing to do with Tom Morris, Alice Walker or Henry Percivale: it was all about him and no-one else - all about Edwin Carlisle and his need for recognition, approval and attention. He went numb with terror as the congregation spoke in unison the words of the service:

...We do earnestly repent and are heartily sorry for these our misdoings; The remembrance of them is grievous unto us; The burden of them is intolerable. Have mercy upon us, Have mercy upon us, most merciful Father...

But Carlisle could decipher no words. All was an echo as the roaring waters in his head crashed again. Pride remained staring at him, mockingly. He tried to look at Alice for an element of comfort, of recognition, of hope, of anything, but her face had changed almost imperceptibly into that of Lucy. His eyes swirled, his breath raced and he stumbled forward slightly. Ragland rose from his pew but was not in time as Carlisle collapsed to the ground to the horror of his congregation.

PART III
THE AFTERMATH
35 YEARS LATER

Truly I tell you, unless you change and become like little children,
you will never enter the kingdom of heaven
Matthew 18:3

The young are taught the vices of the elders, and many who enter
the prison naughty boys, it is feared, leave it accomplished thieves
Joseph Kingsmill, Chaplain of Pentonville Prison, 1852

Tom Morris played with the flower in his fingers. He wanted no other company. It was only a matter of hours since he had laid Carlisle to rest by the side of Martha and Clara and only feet from the grave of Ephraim Ragland. He looked mournfully at the engraving on the headstone in front of him:

Suffer little children, and forbid them not, to come unto me: for of such is the kingdom of heaven.

Carlisle had remained vicar of St Martin's until his death. His health had progressively failed him in his final years, especially after the death of Martha four years before. He had graciously been allowed to remain in the Vicarage even though, for all intents and purposes, the church was run solely by his curate.

It had taken him several years to recover fully from his breakdown, but it was a rather different, meeker and more peaceful Carlisle that had emerged from the darkness. He no longer harboured any intellectual or personal ambition and although he kept half an eye on Pentonville from a distance, he tried, as best he could, to focus his attention on Martha and his parish church, initiating various long-overdue repairs to the church and his marriage. Carlisle no longer wished himself to be a panoptic observer but a humble servant of God, and so he made sure that the altar, not the pulpit, become the focal point of the church in the restoration. To further commemorate this restoration, he donated a large window, above the new main church door, which would later be stained with the Four Evangelists, all keeping a safe eye on the grave of Clara. He also secured the finances required to restore the pews, the chancel, and much of the paraphernalia needed for the Communion. He had taken great pains to make sure that the red and ochre wall images remained and, although fading with each year, they did remain, particularly that of Pride, still silently watching from a lofty height all that entered. He had already abandoned his proposed 'History of St George's Chapel' and although he kept the research and draft chapters that he had already completed, he no longer felt any urge to continue.

Most importantly, perhaps, he sought to make amends to God, and every morning he would pray earnestly for forgiveness. He retained an affectionate eye for those suffering from problems with drink but would never chastise; rather he would often utter a kind word to anyone he saw struggling, administering bread both in Church and in the street by *The George* and *The Swan*. He would so regularly be seen walking this route that the rising part of the track which passed the Vicarage came affectionately to be known as 'Carlisle Rise'. His keen eye for the social welfare of his parishioners was reflected in the many visits he made to their dwellings and the increased amount of bread distributed every Sunday at his own expense. He had instructed Ephraim to restore the almshouses back to their original state, securing permission from his Bishop that one should remain the indefinite dwelling of Tom Morris. The year before he died, barely able to leave the Vicarage due to poor health, he nevertheless exchanged some outlying, unused land with a wealthy landowner to ensure that local farmland was retained under parish control for the benefit and employment of the people of Ruislip. His final, parting gift, shortly before his death, was a peal of eight bells which sang magnificently over the 'Garden of Middlesex,' calling all to Communion and also, poignantly, to his funeral.

Every morning, without fail, he would sit with Clara, his head bowed, but now with thankfulness and hope for he knew she was with him in some way. His rational, intellectual mind had given up trying to understand and he spoke regularly and as openly with her as he did with anyone else. "It was she who freed me from the snare of the hunters," he would often say to himself and to Martha.

Martha never once asked him about Henry's outburst and the suggestions of impropriety towards Lucy (and also, in thought, towards Alice) and Carlisle never once raised the issue. He had sought to make amends to Alice by confessing his sins privately in his Journal and, in the same way, also sought amends from his congregation, many of whom were disillusioned and dismayed by the events of Lent 1843. Carlisle had kept his Journal locked in his study drawer so as to keep secret his innermost thoughts and feelings, and for a time had even considered burning it and using the ashes to impose the sign of the cross during Lent, thus turning his turmoil into something productive and holy at last. Ultimately, though, he had placed it carefully in a tight leather casing and, early one morning, along with the diary which had been bequeathed to him before the start of the experiment, buried it secretly under the earth which now formed part of the new, restored south aisle - a way of laying to rest, he hoped, the disquiet of his heart.

Immediately after the experiment, Henry had been released from service by Mr Ansell the blacksmith, who had finally lost patience with his drunkenness and abusive behaviour. Henry had remained around Ruislip for a few weeks afterwards, picking up odd jobs in one farm after the next, but as his manual skills became less and less needed and his drunkenness more and more serious, he finally exhausted all possibilities of employment and lodging and so one morning had taken off to London and had not been seen since. Some unverified rumours said that he himself had ended up in prison; others reported that he had been seen begging by the Woolwich docks. The majority, though, did not have a care about him and as soon as his name was mentioned it was forgotten or else remembered only very briefly and with little warmth.

Percivale's vacant position was given to Stanley Hawkins, Ansell's apprentice, who had unwittingly set in motion the spiral that led to Percivale's confession. Fate worked Her magic once more and Hawkins, a naïve, yet loyal, young lad, became a welcome partner to Alice, who had been retained by Martha as a domestic aide after the experiment ended. Martha treated her as the daughter she had never seen develop into a young woman. In turn, Alice found the mother figure she had never really experienced. Alice remained at the Vicarage until her marriage to Hawkins and, through some parish connections, Carlisle secured for them both a small, clean dwelling a mile or so from Ruislip. Hawkins naturally fell into Ansell's position upon the latter's death eight years later and, as Alice became blessed with love, care, security and two beautiful little girls, so Martha was blessed with the role of a doting surrogate grandmother.

Peter was nowhere to be seen at either his mother's or father's funeral. He had cut all ties with his family early on before embarking upon a life of crime that took him throughout Britain and Europe. Rumours were rife that he made it as far as America. It was, in many ways, the final death knell for Carlisle when his youngest son was formally sentenced to eleven years' penal servitude shortly before his father's death. Carlisle blamed himself, naturally, for Peter's errant ways: he had shown little interest in his development as a child and his mourning for Clara had prevented his son from having a meaningful father figure in his life in the crucial stages of his development. In a spate of rebellion, Peter pursued a military rather than an academic or ecclesiastical career and soon started to fall foul of the law. Until his eventual capture and conviction his misdemeanours were largely kept from his parents by his use of aliases, which apparently were legion.

If there was a crumb of consolation for Carlisle before he died, it was that developments at Pentonville and other prisons had led to a fairer and less intimidating experience for the prisoners, their mental well-being being taken far more seriously. The vehement and aggressive spiritual bullying of James Ralph had lasted little more than a year before Lord Wharncliffe had terminated his services and handed the spiritual baton over to Joseph Kingsmill. The effort of it all clearly took its toll on Wharncliffe, who entered little into public life after that and died almost three years to the day Pentonville opened, on December 19, 1845. Kingsmill, although in favour of the separate system espoused by Ralph and criticised by Wharncliffe, was less foreboding than his predecessor and advocated a softer 'law of kindness' to those in separate confinement. Public opinion remained mixed, with those of a certain education and background agreeing with the description given by *The Times* that the early regime at Pentonville was simply a 'maniac-making system.'

Kingsmill openly remarked that his correspondence with Carlisle, especially in the wake of the suicide of Harry Flynn and other cases of mental insanity, had been a catalyst for the various prison reforms of 1848 and 1853, which saw a reduction in the length of separate confinement for prisoners and initiated accelerated release for good behaviour. Meaningful employment was also introduced, rather than the futile and soul-destroying oakum-picking to which many were subject. Yet, by and large, the Home Office continued to support the separate system and panoptic radial design and by 1856 two-thirds of British prisons were either built or altered to accommodate such a system, which sought to punish and deter, rather than to reform and rehabilitate.

Kingsmill remained openly critical of the treatment that Ralph had received from the so-called 'benevolent theorists' who had first suggested the Pentonville experiment to the British government, claiming that they sought to undermine the religious principle on which the separate system was founded. Ralph's reputation had suffered greatly after his dismissal and Kingsmill, who retained great respect for his mentor, spoke passionately and genuinely at Ralph's funeral in 1855 with the aim of restoring to him in death the respect that he failed to achieve in life: "a Christian warrior, fighting the good fight of faith, with all his armour on, his sword firmly grasped, and his face towards the enemy." Ill health had been a frequent companion of Kingsmill as the years went by and he was forced to spend considerable time away from prison and hand over more duties to his own assistant, Rev. John Burt. He died in 1865, shortly before the latest Prison Reform Act, which brought transportation to Tasmania to a close two years later.

Carlisle had often confided in Ragland about his despair over Peter's plight. "A man is his own man, sir," Ragland would often say to try and assuage Carlisle of his biting guilt. "A man is his own man." Carlisle appreciated the kindness of his sexton and was plunged into further mourning when Ragland fell to pneumonia at the age of seventy-one, all this time having remained as his sexton. With no-one to fulfil Ragland's grave-digging role, Tom Morris, who had been free from intoxication since the 'experiment', had undertaken the bitter task and it seemed a natural progression for Tom to replace Ephraim as church sexton, a role he now filled with gratitude and ability.

Tom played with the flower again, watching it intertwine with his grimy fingers. Above him hung the green of the yew and the holly, an ever-present reminder of survival among the decay that covered the graveyard. He felt it very apt that the old yew tree shaded the grave of the Carlisles from the elements: the summer sun, which now beat down fiercely, and the winter snow, which clung to its leaves like needy children. To his right, the noise of life's bustle reminded him that the 'cell' he occupied thirty-five years ago was now his home and that the five families who occupied the remaining almshouses, all of which had a large brood of hungry offspring, were now his neighbours. Tom smiled to himself as he remembered those thirty days which had, without exaggeration, changed his life. His fondness for Carlisle had grown daily and although he had struggled with the more theological aspects of the 'experiment' he had developed a practical understanding of his reliance on drink and of the spiritual void in his life which he had been trying to fill. So much so that, in his will, Carlisle had bequeathed to him, as a symbolic token, his precious annotated copy of *Spiritual Exercises*, along with his children's book of Biblical stories.

To the left of where Tom sat, and where many times in the past he had vomited due to inebriation, a soft yellow carpet of flowers now lay. He stood up and brushed the earth from his trousers, taking care not to damage the delicate flower. He slowly walked up the path towards the entrance of the church. He entered, out of the direct sunlight and into the shade. He looked over at the bread basket and recalled the time (one of many) when he had sought refuge in the church because of his intoxication. Now it was his duty to make sure the bread was delivered and administered every Sunday, under directions issued by Carlisle before his death, and he undertook the role with care and joy. He was unsure how his relationship with the new vicar, Rev. Dartington, would be and he was careful not to expect too much: his relationship with Carlisle could never be replicated, nor would he want it to be. Like Ephraim Ragland, he would go about his business as sexton quietly and humbly, in fond remembrance of his former vicar.

"Papa can't see me, Papa can't find me!" laughed a voice suddenly and Tom looked up, smiling. Peeking out from behind one of the octagonal columns of the nave was the face of a young girl of five. Tom looked towards her with an intense feeling of love and gratitude. He had married late in life, at the age of fifty-eight, but the result was worth an eternal wait. He crept up slowly and playfully to the column and grabbed the little girl in his arms, swinging her around and kissing her half a dozen times. "Papa has found you!" he laughed, and she laughed too. "Is that for me?" she asked, looking at the yellow flower still preserved in his hand. "Yes, a pretty flower for *my* pretty flower," he replied, handing the precious gift to her. She smelt it and then gently placed it behind her ear. "I love you, Papa!" she said, hugging him again. He grasped her hand tightly and walked with her towards the church door. "I love you too, my dear child. I love you too," he spoke tenderly as he looked up at the new window donated by Carlisle and smiled. He locked the door firmly behind him and gazed affectionately at his daughter as, hand in hand, they walked back into the open air.

THE END

Printed in Great Britain
by Amazon

40391541R00086